T0159082

THE
MEMPHIS
BAT

M. J. REISEN

authorHOUSE®

AuthorHouse™
1663 Liberty Drive
Bloomington, IN 47403
www.authorhouse.com
Phone: 1 (800) 839-8640

Published by AuthorHouse   09/15/2016

ISBN: 978-1-5246-4005-7 (sc)
ISBN: 978-1-5246-4006-4 (hc)
ISBN: 978-1-5246-4004-0 (e)

Library of Congress Control Number: 2016915392

Print information available on the last page.

Contents

1

◇

Two Damsels

L loyd Brick's square-jawed face is a mask of repressed fury. His normally even brows are coagulated into a bank of thunderheads over eyes flickering with ire. He emits a plume of smoke from his hand-rolled cigarette across the page of a letter in a gesture of defiance. As if the vapor could dissolve the vexatious nature of the dispatch. But, the characters remain stubbornly in the form of an informal invitation from the D.A.'s office for 'a little chat'.

Almost two years, two Silver Stars and a Purple Heart ago, he decided that his degree from Carnegie Mellon in urban sociology combined with his experience in the military would afford him a chance to administer his own sense of justice to a world which had just pulled itself back from the brink of an authoritarian abyss.

But, the compromises he made in establishing the firm were proving to be a double edged sword which now seemed to be quivering in the air above him. And it hung on the thin thread of his partner's character. And now, more than ever; his own.

Brick had no illusions about the comportment of any police force in any city in America. But, in the new post-war America, anyone who was under the impression that things could still operate as if it were the Barbary Coast were in for a rude awakening. In the ten years since both the Golden Gate and Bay bridges were opened within six months of each other, with millions of citizens reintegrating into a peace-time civilization, it would

1

be unseemly for the city to continue to indulge in it's former provincial tendencies in this country that just fought for universal freedom again for the second time in the century.

His partner's no-nonsense reputation in regards to the handling of San Francisco's criminal population and his long tenure in the SFPD helped to establish many connections in City Hall which afforded them both access and a certain amount of accommodation. But, along with the post-war expansion, a desire to see the city become more genteel in it's reputation was making the more problematic procedures of local law enforcement increasingly untenable.

Men like his partner kept the streets safe in war time. But, word gets around with so many more and new mouths and ears in circulation. Doubt creeps in everywhere and business falls off. And the deterioration of his partner's professional behavior has extended to his personal life as well. His drinking, gambling and extra-marital episodes have all become open secrets. There were even the rumors of a black market scandal.

Brick, all alone in an empty office at the end of a workday, thinks back; except for a strong arm eviction and a careless case of adultery, there had been no clients in almost two months. And things had become tenuous before that. And just today, his normally reliable secretary had called to say she would be delayed because of a 'family emergency'. Brick slips the letter back into it's envelope and curses himself for an indolent fool for not having addressed all this sooner. At this rate he may as well jump off the Golden Gate. Over sixty other fed up souls had done so by now.

The metallic crunch of the key in the lock of the corridor-door office lurches his revere to the present and he slides the letter into a drawer with more missives of misfortune: overdue bills, even a few collection letters. Just as he shuts the drawer, the door to the inner office swings open to reveal his secretary, Lorna Christy; small, nubile, with wiry blond hair and a spray of freckles across the bump on her nose only adding to her appeal.

Still in her hat and blue box coat, she gasps,"Oh good, you *are* here." She closes the door firmly behind her and crosses to Brick's desk,"I need to ask a huge favor, boss."

"I'm sure you're owed a few," he admits somewhat ruefully.

She leans on the corner of the desk,"My cousin, Eugene is a JG aboard the U.S.S. *Clamp.*"

"She's salvage, right?" Brick asks.

Lorna nods,"They've been towing vessels to Mare Island and … Hunter's Point." She frowns and looks away. Brick leans forward, and rests his forearms on the desk," Something to do with what's going on in the Marshall's, I take it," he stubs out his butt.

Lorna nods again and her right hand reaches across her body and worries her left elbow. The gold sword-shaped pin on her blouse winks in the dim afternoon light."Anyway, while they were inspecting one vessel, he came across – found something he knew didn't belong there."

Brick tugs at an earlobe," And this 'something' is what the 'family emergency' was all about."

She nods again and glances at the office door before she speaks,"What I know is; he found this object: a jar made of stone, sealed, with Egyptian hieroglyphics etched on it." Brick starts slightly, but she forestalls him,"You're not the only one with a college education, if he says they're Egyptian, then you can be pretty sure -"

He holds up a hand in surrender," Fine. So, he finds what appears to be an ancient canopic jar almost half a world away from where it started. It's the Navy's property and mystery now."

Lorna drops her head and quarter turns from the desk, but leans against it, "Umm…."

Brick moans and leans back in his chair,"What…"

She lifts her face to him and explains, earnestly,"He's not a thief Lloyd, he was just so excited about what he found, that he had to find out if it was real – what he thought it was before he …" She sighs and drops her gaze again,"Anyway, he brought it back and gave it to an old professor of his at Berkeley to get his opinion on it and…."

Her head drops again and lower lip tucked under her incisors, she continues in a low, strained tone,"Someone stole it."

"Someone," he leans forward, both palms land on the desk. She becomes animated again,"Yes, and that 'someone' injured poor Professor Wonderly in the act. Please, Lloyd, my cousin didn't mean any harm and now this thing has gotten serious and if the Navy were to find out, it would be -"

She breaks off sharply and stares hard down at her fingers now picking agitatedly at the edges of the blotter on his desk. Small flakes of tobacco ash tumble and skitter across the surface, she starts to smooth them towards the still full ashtray when he reaches out and grasps her hand,"You're not the maid, angel, you're my right arm. Tell me all about it."

Lorna takes in a shuddering breath, smooths her hair back over her left ear and smiles tremulously at Diamond,"Thank you, Lloyd." She adds quickly and fervently," And please, not a word of this to Walter. I honestly don't know if he can be -"

"That goes without saying,"he scowls. "Now before his nibs deigns to show up, when did this robbery take place?" He leans over, picks up the astray and dumps the contents into his wastepaper basket. The leans down, pulls open the second drawer down and removes a cigar box and sets it on the desk.

"Last night. Eugene came over to tell me all about it. I read him the riot act regarding 'chain of command', but in the end, what's done is done; he's my cousin and where else could I turn?"

"And the police haven't been informed? Even the campus cops?" From the box he removes a tobacco pouch and a sheaf of cigarette paper.

"No, my cousin convinced the Professor that taking their position into account it was best not to get the authorities involved until he could talk to me."

"Because you work for me." She nods sheepishly. "Well, so far, so good. And the Professor, was he hospitalized?" Brick asks as he smooths out the tobacco and folds the paper over with his forefingers rolling over his thumbs on each end of the twist.

She shakes her head,"Eugene took him to be treated at the campus infirmary. I don't know exactly what he told them, but thankfully he doesn't seem to have been seriously injured."

Brick nods in acknowledgment just as they hear the door to the reception area open and close. They share a knowing glance. Lorna straightens up, wipes at her eyes with her fingers, tosses her hair back, strides to the office door and opens it to reveal the senior partner of the firm – Walter Diamond.

His frame filled most of the doorway as he stood, one hand reaching for the doorknob, the other cradling his wet fedora. He gives Lorna an ironic little bow and then strides into the room, flinging his hat on the coat rack," Your feminine intuition is solid as always." He shrugs off his overcoat and proceeds to hang it under his hat.

Lorna gives him a side-long gander as she leans on the doorknob,"You're right. I can tell all ready, I'm not likely to get paid again this Friday." And with one more shared glare with Brick, she slowly swings herself out of the room, closing the door behind her.

Diamond smiles tightly after her,"And we haven't fired her, because...?"

"You have to pay me first!"comes the not too muffled reply from the other side of the door.

Brick smiles and even Diamond guffaws with appreciation as he turns to the window. Thumbs tucked in his vest pockets, fingers splayed out over his expanding midriff, he stares out over the Embarcadero. Brick's face falls as he takes in his partner's back. He reaches for the drawer with the reproaching documents, but stops when what might be a version of 'En Cuba' warbles through the room with some sibilance from his partner's lips.

Brick tilts his head and clocks his partner's dark blue Botany suit all the way down to the gleaming brown Freeman's. The gray-white hair freshly curried and the only hint of alcohol seems to be bay rum aftershave on his beefy face. He drops his hands into his pockets and the jingling of change takes on a ragged rhythmic accompaniment.

Brick withdraws his hand and reaches for the smoke in the ashtray instead. This sudden show of politesse tickles his antennae. Such an ostentatious display could only mean a reversal of fortune. Now it was up to him to find out at what cost," If I didn't know you'd better, and I do, I'd say you look like a man who's looking for his ship to come in."

Diamond stops whistling and chuckles,"Or maybe just waiting to cast off." He goes back to his tuneless trill, steps closer to the window and casts his gaze down towards the street. Brick stares hard at the older man. For a year now he has been far too willing to let him also occupy the 'senior' position in the firm, no questions asked. Past time to turn his skills to his own house.

"Taking Ava on a cruise to set her heart at ease?" He says this lightly and leans back in is chair, confident of his opening gambit. Sure enough, his partner stops whistling, but remains fixed at the window,"She gets seasick." He brings his right hand out of his pocket and flicks apart the Venetian blinds.

"Shouldn't be surprised, with the rough waters she's been through lately," Brick offers as casually as before. "Cry me a river. If she was truly unhappy, she would leave. It's a free country," his partner responds as he drops his hand and returns it to his trouser maraca. "Never having been married, you wouldn't know how it works, like I do."

Brick leans back in his chair and squints at his partner through the cigarette smoke,"I wasn't aware that marriage liked you. Or vice versa." His partner replies again without turning,"Don't mistake my infidelity for insincerity." Brick inspects his cigarette butt carefully as he rolls it between his fingers,"The frequency of your insincerity is no mistake."

"If you are really that concerned why don't you take your evidence to her. I'm sure she'll be glad to be our first paying client in over a month," he turns from the window and before Brick can launch a rejoinder he adds,"I'm being shadowed."

Brick pauses, his fingers slowly crackle the cigarette paper. He then asks carelessly,"Since when?" Diamond shrugs,"Since this morning. Don't see them now."

"Them?", Brick scratches his jaw. Could the Feds have a file already? More likely his most recent transgressions have come home to roost,"Lima's boys?" he offers. Diamond snorts in derision,"That was unworthy of you. You know Tony doesn't skulk. He insists." Brick flushes at the dispraise, but shrugs,"Perhaps a loose confederation of suspicious husbands or maybe they're just interested in your tailor."

"You flatter me," he crosses to his desk and sits,"A Mutt and Jeff. Spied them both enough to not believe in the coincidence. Don't see them now." He leans back in his chair, folds his hands behind his head and turns slightly to face towards the windows. Brick leans forward, stubs out his cigarette and is about take a more invasive tact of interrogation when a soft knock comes on the door followed by Lorna who twirls animatedly into the room and quickly, but gently closes the door behind her and leans on it as she pronounces:"There's a young lady to see you. Maybe I'll get that paycheck after all."

Diamond's chair creaks as he turns back from the window and his hands move to straighten his tie,"Well, shoo her in, doll, shoo her in." Their secretary's face holds a mischievous smile as she opens the door, and nods for the unseen guest to enter,"Won't you come in, Miss Daeva?"

Her approach was demure, thanking the secretary so softly that it couldn't have been louder than the scrape of wasp wings, but there seemed to be an aura that preceded her so that the men could feel the pressure change in the room as she entered. Through the lambent slashes thrown on the floor by the Venetian blinds, one could see she was wrapped strategically in red satin, each drape accentuating her pliant curves. Her face is tantalizingly concealed under a veil from a burgundy hat with a turned up brim balanced out by an arc of feathers on the opposite side.

Although no taller than Lorna, she was smaller boned and her skin had a sub-cutaneous luster that hinted at origins of a more ancient and exotic clime. She takes small, hesitant steps as she looks from one man to the other. Both men rise from their seats. Lorna beams an expectant grin at Brick as   Diamond maneuvers an oaken armchair into place closer to his desk than to Brick's. The veil leaves her mouth exposed and a small smile flits across the gleaming fruit of her lips. She emits a soft,"Thank you" and reveals small, even, alabaster teeth over an elegantly cleft chin. She slips sinuously into the proffered seat, but remains at the edge, hands folded over the small purse in her lap.

"Now, what is it we would be more than pleased to do for you Miss.... Daeva?," Diamond said, barely suppressing a leer. Brick scowls at his partner as he re-seats himself, but on the corner of his desk, close to the new client.

"Mm. Thank you. This is very difficult, I - ". She drops her hand and twists open the small clutch bag in her lap and pinches out a small handkerchief. The air becomes immediately redolent with an musty, earthy scent. Diamond half rises from his seat and offers in an avuncular tone,"Just tell us all about it from the beginning. We'll know what to do once we get the lay of the land." He looks pointedly at his partner. Brick nods in concurrence.

She nods and excuses herself,"I-I'm sorry, I – it's just so upsetting -" She pauses again and dabs the linen towards her face to stave off tears. Brick gauges the accent: the slight hesitation in cadence, the minute lingering on the vowels; some eastern influence.

"I don't know how this got started or where, but she's supposedly here now with him and if I cannot get her to return to New York with me before our parent's return home from vacation, I just don't know what I'll…. You see, she's only seventeen and I know we've never been as close as sister's perhaps should be, but I am responsible and father will kill her if he ever finds out -"

All of this comes out in a jagged rush and to calm her and keep her focused, Brick raises his hand and interjects,"When do they get back?"

"In two weeks. She was supposed to be at school, but they called me and said she'd been absent for three days straight – I live in the city. And then just as I was thinking of calling the police, her letter showed up in the mail telling me she had runaway with this, this… man. And then I wasn't sure what to do or who to turn to." She twists the silk in her hands a little more then continues,"I sent a telegram asking her to come home. General Delivery was the only address she would give. Then I became frantic when I didn't hear back and sent word that I was coming, because I was so worried. I probably shouldn't have done that, should I?"

Brick takes his turn at consolation,"It isn't always easy to know what to do. Especially with family." He took advantage of his nearness and leans on the desk with an encouraging smile. "So, you've been here how long and still no luck?"

"Three days. I wrote her again, telling her I'd be at the St. Mark's and to at least, please, come and talk to me even if I couldn't persuade her to come home. But, no word…. it's been so terrible waiting and not knowing what might be happening to her and not being able to – to…."

Both men frown and nod sympathetically as she tails off with a small defeated gesture, daubs at he nose and continues,"I decided to write a letter to General Delivery and last evening went to the Post Office. I didn't see her, but I did see…. him." Her eyes dropped as did the volume of her voice.

"Him", Diamond says almost dreamily, eyes half-closed and slowly blinking. She nods and looks up,"Louis Pines. He would only tell me that she was fine, that they were happy and that she didn't want to see me and I should just go back to New York. But, how can I without knowing if he's telling the truth?"

Brick asks,"How did you leave it?"

"He said that even if she didn't come that he would just to make sure I was on my way with a 'clear conscience' about my sister's welfare, as he put it." For the first time he voice took on an edge of anger instead of despair. Brick nods at his partner,"We shouldn't have any trouble with this."

Diamond gives a snort of derision and shakes his head. Brick continues,"It's simply a matter of having a man shadow him when he leaves the hotel to return to your sister. If she does come with him and you can persuade her to leave, so much the better. If, on the other hand, they seem reluctant to part -"

"We got ways of managing that!" his partner interjects roughly. Brick frowns at Diamond, but grunts in assent. Their prospective client suddenly claps a hand to her chest,"Oh, but you must be careful! I'm very afraid of what he might do to her if – I mean her being underage and all, mightn't he do something desperate to save himself?"

"Maybe. But if he's smart, he'll do anything to -"

"We know how to handle him," his partner intrudes again."You can trust us to take care of everything."

"I do trust you," she says avidly as she reaches up and rolls back the veil to reveal: eyes large, generous, dark. Almond shaped, they flash an amber hue as she turns to take both men in with her imploring gaze. Her lashes are a thick fringe that reiterate the pitch of her irises. "But, I want you to know that he's a very dangerous man. Why, I'm honestly terrified he might even kill Jeanie, if he thought it could save him."

"Were any threats made, either way?," Brick asks. She shakes her head,"I told him that I wanted nothing more than to get my sister home before my parents had found out what she'd done and that I'd never breathe a word to a living soul about him if he helped me convince her to return. Although..." She looks down "I did say that if Papa ever *did* find out that he wouldn't stop until he was properly punished. Perhaps, I shouldn't have."

"Can he cover up by marrying her?", Diamond asks. Brick crosses behind his desk and reaches for a pencil and a pad of paper.

The question appears to fluster her,"I – oh, I don't think so he has a - a wife and three children somewhere back east. That - that's what Jeannie wrote when she told me why she ran off with him."

Brick leans on the desk," What does he look like?"

"Oh, he's tall, taller than you, but – gangly, is how I think you would say. Dark hair, thick eyebrows, in fact quite hairy, he seemed to have a few days growth of beard on him. Prominent nose, a wide mouth, he barks in a loud, sharp voice and has a very rough manner. He gives the impression of – he comes across as a violent person."

"Any other distinguishing features? Eye color, scars...?"

"Mm", she put her fingers up to her lips,"his eyes are a very peculiar color, almost... yellow. He was wearing a light gray suit and gray hat when I saw him."

Brick finishes scribbling,"What does he do for a living?"

Again she pauses, uncertain,"I…. don't know." She shakes her head."I haven't the slightest idea."

"What time is the meeting set for?"

"He said eight or a little after."

"Fine, we'll have a man there. It'll help if you meet Pines in the lobby."

"I'll look after it myself,"Diamond says as he stands up and sticks his thumb to his chest.

"Yes, very well. Oh -" She starts and fumbles open her small handbag, only this time the air is filled with the bouquet of new bills, totaling two hundred dollars. "Will that be enough?" She asks as she holds the money out.

"Absolutely," Diamond replies as he plucks the bills avidly from her hand. "And you don't need to look for me. I'll see you all right."

She rises and holds her hand out to both in turn,"Thank you, thank you," they bow slightly over her extended hand as they take it. She crosses to the door, Brick follows her and opens it for her. She turns in the doorway,"You gentlemen have done me an invaluable service." Lorna rises from behind her desk where she is busy tap-tapping away on her typewriter and shows the enthralling new client out.

As Brick turns back into the room and closes the door, his partner is snapping one of the bills critically between his outstretched hands,"They're right enough," he says as he slips one of the bills into his vest pocket. "And they've got bothers in her bag." He barks a mirthless laugh, pats his broad belly and teeters back on his heels,"Should've spoken up son. What's the matter? Your war wound slowin' you down?"

Brick scowls at the provocative mention of his affliction; a head wound which had him unconscious for three days. He still experiences occasional 'spells'. They had been decreasing in intensity and frequency over the last months, but the past week had seen three mild occurrences and it didn't take a psychic or a physician to tell him that a major modification in circumstances could only be advantageous.

Even if he were to have to relocate to the Tendernob district and take his chances alone. But, then, although the city may have tossed out the low-life element in '17, that kind of stain doesn't wash out cleanly. Half dozen blocks east of Nob Hill, the neighborhood was still treated with disdain and suspicion. Which is why it was easy to make rent every month.

"What? And deprive you of a chance to once again prove your '*sin*cerity?'", he said as he pocketed the remaining money and took his seat behind his desk.

"Always thinking of others," his partner replies with an oleaginous smile. He plucks his watch fob from his vest and consults his timepiece,"Oops! And speaking of others, I'm gonna be late for an appointment." He crosses to the window and peers through the blinds again and mutters,"Damn!" He turns from the window, his face redder than usual with consternation until he spies the coat rack.

With a sly grin he crosses to the rack and starts to shrug on Brick's coat.

"What the hell -", Brick starts to object. His partner continues on, placing Brick's hat on his head,"I need you to run interference for me; looks like Jeff is back on the clock." He plucks his own accoutrement from the stand and holds them out towards Brick, expectantly who seethes, but slowly accepts the garments as he asks,"You're sure this won't affect your delicate plans for the evening?"

Diamond crosses to the door opens it and turns,"Of course not. What makes you think I'd ever disappoint a lady, let alone a client?" With a tip of the hat he backs out,"Thanks, partner. I'll go out the back way. Get these back to you tomorrow, if not sooner." And with that he exits, humming tunelessly,"I need no shackles to remind me, I'm just a prisoner of love..." And with that he is gone.

Brick stands looking after him. Still bristling, he places his partner's hat on his head and slips into the slightly too short trench coat. Lorna has stopped typing and also stares at the door, then turns to her employer,"Suppose I told you that his meeting is in Chinatown?"

Brick snaps,"I'd say, I should hang up my gumshoes and hire a harem of Mata Haris' to run down their high heels while I desk jockey and golf three days a work week." And with that he slams out the office door.

Lorna glowers after him,"Women get results. We proved that in the last war." She slaps at the typewriter carriage returning it and begins typing again, her fingers irritably punching the keys.

Brick bundles outside. Although sunset was still over an hour away, the tufted marine layer that wreathed well inland at this hour brought twilight early to the peninsula and would only aid in his cozenage. Keeping his collar up and brim down, he passes the late Gothic revival arches of the California Commercial Wool building and makes his way southwest along Sutter Street. He keeps his hands hunched in his pockets and his eyes constantly probing as he strides purposefully through the evening crowd.

He just approaches the intersection of Sutter and Grant when he registers a small bundle of a figure pacing him at half a block distance. He turns right on Grant then right again on Campton Place as he angles for the northeast corner of Union Square. While waiting at the corner of Post and Stockton for a traffic light change, he makes sure his shadow is keeping pace. He almost smiles to himself as he notes his trundling tail try to keep up as he crosses the street and enters the world's first underground parking garage.

Once inside the garage he breaks into a short sprint and conceals himself around the corner to the next level down. He waits, quieting his breath, when he sees a lump of a shadow approach, stop, waver and then reverse course; shambling off with what sounds like mumbled curses. He gives the shade a few minutes to create some distance. "I thought he said it was the 'Jeff' member of the tandem", he thought as he then heads for the corner exit at Geary and Powell.

Back out onto street level, he jogs across Powell Street to the entrance of the St. Francis Hotel. Once under the awning he cases the street behind him to make sure the coast is clear, then ducks into the lobby. Pushing through the revolving doors, he turns immediately to the left past the reception desk. Gene LeBret, the hotel detective looks up as he approaches. Brick puts his finger to his lips as he passes his fellow flatfoot and LeBret nods in acquiescence then moves towards the front to cover his exit to Geary Street.

Once back outside Brick takes a cursory glance around and decides to keep heading south. It is dinner time now, especially if one considers a cocktail beforehand. At Powell and Ellis he turns left, crosses the street and heads for the green awning of John's Grill. A boxcar and an order of chops, potatoes and sliced tomatoes later, Brick is accentuating his tobacco intake with a hot caffeinated beverage when he comes to some brief conclusions on the day's events.

While he could probably trust his life to his secretary, asking to extend that allowance to others, even her relatives was only asking for more trouble than it was probably worth. Which begs an important question: if Lorna's cousin is such an upstanding citizen, what was it about his find that kept him from reporting it to military authority?

And the other client: while her case wasn't an extraordinary one, the same adjective definitely could not be applied to herself. An aura proceed and surrounded her with a beguiling appeal, that while anchored in her beauty was more than just attractiveness. In fact, it was only now that Brick started to feel the effects of her presence start to dissipate from his mind like so much tobacco smoke. "More like opium", he assesses as he downs the last of his coffee, rubs his forehead and eyes and extricates himself from the booth to collect 'his' coat and hat.

The marine layer had given way to a full fledged fog bank as he slowly makes his way back to Union Square. He is thinking of checking in with LeBret at the St. Francis to see if he spotted the tail and then catch a cab to his apartment on Lombard. Just as he approaches the corner of Powell and Geary, a figure approaches him casually out of the darkness,"Say, bud. Got a match?"

Before Brick can get his hands from his pockets, the tall stranger snatches the hat off of his own head with his left hand and plunges it into Brick's face following it up with a stiff right cross. Brick tumbles back into the arms of another assailant and finds his arms being pinned. The first thug drives his fists into Brick's midsection, one-two-three knocking out his wind. They drag him into the nearest doorway where they thrust him against the wall.

An elbow is shoved under his chin and cracks his head against stone. One voice growls:"It seems you got something that very important and impatient people want. I suggest you -"

"Hey, hey, I don't think he – what the hell? Who're, what the hell...?" the second voice sputters as Brick slides down the wall into a black pool of unconsciousness that opens at his feet. Before he completely immerses, he is aware of a scuffle which buffets him once more against the wall and he fades out.

2

Death in the Fog

A ll is dark. In the background, he senses a slow, almost subsonic drone in counterpoint with a high-pitched gibberish. The cacophony resembles two tape recorders playing at the same time at opposite speeds. The drone sensation becomes a throbbing which he now can recognize as coming from his cranium and the treble noise subsides to a rhythmic static.

The exterior sound softens into a liquid spattering. Lifting his head, he picks up the scent of something with an earthy, mossy bouquet. Then the odor fades in the shifting beads of moisture in the night air. He opens his eyes, and doing his best not to moves he casts his gaze about to discover that he is lying prone, with his hands folded over his chest and cradling his hat. He turns his head slightly to his right and regards two wooden doors set with barred windows. Rolling his head painfully to the left he makes out an arched doorway. He closes his eyes and starts to move his hands when:

"Is this what you spent all those years at that fancy college for?"

Brick groans in pain and recognition. He slowly levers himself up on his left elbow,"Well, I'm pretty sure this is from your school of hard knocks. Thanks."

"You've always needed toughening up. Look at the way you've handled business... and my clothes," he crouches down and seems to take in Brick's condition a little more closely, but keeps his distance. Brick now recognizes the fluid cadence as rain. It glistens behind the figure, keeping all features in the shadow.

"Well, ya got me there. Letting you run the show has got us where we are today," Brick wipes his mouth and spits in his partner's general direction. He can taste blood.

"I'm here to do you a solid and this is how you treat me?" comes the incredulous response.

"Oh, right. Everything has been for my own good, all along. Did you dynamite the client tonight, too?" Brick asks as he gathers his legs under him.

His partner looks off before answering, casting his profile against the cold night's drizzle,"Things didn't go exactly as planned. So, I'm here to tell you kid; forget her. She's out of your league."

Brick feels his anger beginning to overwhelm his pain; with a groan he sits up,"And here you are touting your success, obviously. You old -"

"I mean it, kid!" he barks. His head snaps back so fast, moisture flies off his hat brim. He stands quickly and steps slightly back.

Brick looks up at his partner coldly,"Just give me a hand and a drink and then we'll see who gets to tell who, what." He reaches out with one hand while clutching the hat in the other. The other figure remains stolid. Then after a few moments, he pulls a hand out and extends it in Brick's direction,"Reach for it."

Brick almost laughs, then launches himself at the proffered hand, ready to use it as leverage, not just to get up but to -

'KLANG'

He recoils in pain, cradling his right fist in his left hand. After squeezing it under his armpit and shaking out the pain he tries to examine it in the dim light. He staggers out to the side walk and looks up at the building and spies two mullioned windows overhead then casts his gaze down the street to make out the street sign: Maiden Lane. How did he get all the way across the square?

He drops his eyes to spy the object he struck: a fire hydrant pipe extending from the building, slick with water. He touches the pipe to ensure it's solidity, then slumps against the wall. Where did his partner go? Who were those men? What happened to them and – him? This couldn't all be related to his head wound, could it?

Trembling, he passes his hand several times over his face then spies his partner's hat on the ground. He bends gingerly bends down, scoops it up and slaps rain water off of it and lurches along to the intersection at Grant Avenue, occasionally righting himself with the closest wall.

He reaches the street and leans against the nearest building and tries to brace himself with some deep breaths, but his aching ribs bring him up short. He carefully places the little-too-large hat on his head, then slowly limps up the street on legs that feel like toothpicks.

He reaches his office building on Sutter Street. Built on the site of the old Lick Hotel, it is the only one in the city with it's own unique blend of French Renaissance and Romanesque architecture. The location was a conscious decision in regards to the choice reputation they hoped to the agency to project. His gait is stiff, and he discovers blood on the back of is shirt-collar by the time he reaches the revolving doors.

Brick slumps against the frieze between the two glass doors and gives the set on the left a few resounding thumbs with the side of his fist. In a few minutes a dim light skitters through the lobby to the entrance. As the light scrapes across Brick and there is a jangle of keys as the nightwatchman unlocks the door.

Brick pushes through and leaves a smear of blood on the glass as he practically stumbles into the arms of the plump attendant. "Mr. Brick, are you -" he catches the shamus as he stumbles to one knee and pulls back a crimson palm. "Oh, Mr. Brick," he gasps. "I'll call Doctor -"

"Just get me to my feet and to my office, Joel. And get my secretary on the line, will you?"

The stout Egyptian looks doubtfully at Brick, but levers himself under the detective's left arm and helps him across the lobby to the elevators. Brick surreptitiously glances around at the marble, the painted ceiling and exposed beams. All of which seemed to emanate a singular cold as if the building's ornate facade ceased to mask the chill of a city used to keeping order, but not necessarily the law.

Thirty-nine minutes later, Brick is leaning against the door frame between the reception area and his office when a shadow looms across the frosted glass of the outer door, etched with the name of their firm. He watches the doorknob turn, bloodied towel in hand.

Lorna stands in the doorway, peering out from under a dripping, floppy hat brim. Her slightly puckered brow holds a question. The rest of her face gives him no purchase. He crosses from the doorway, bloody towel in hand,"Thanks for coming in after hours angel, you're a good man."

He starts to sway a little and she helps him into a chair in the waiting area. She emits a groan somewhere between exasperation and concern and efficiently checks his pulse and pupils. Satisfied, she probes his scalp through his matted brown hair and pronounces,"Not as bad as it looks, and lucky for you, I have some butterfly bandages in my desk kit."

She moves quickly to her desk while peeling off her hat, coat and gloves all of which she dumps in a pile on her chair and disappears as she bends down behind the desk to access the bottom drawer.

"Of course you do," Brick sighs as he sprawls back in the chair and returns the towel to his head. "The flow has pretty much stopped now."

Lorna pops up with a tackle box which she plops on the desktop and proceeds to rummage through, bringing out gauze, scissors and tape,"Well, let's just stay on the safe side …. say-" She stops suddenly and looks up at him with apprehension,"Have you been having…? I mean is this because -"

"Couldn't be your case, I haven't had a chance to – oh, you meant…." he stops and briefly lifts the towel from his head,"This had nothing to do with my wound."

She starts to cut strips of tape and roll out gauze,"Then tell me what happened, or should we hire an investigator?"

"Hilarious. Would you get my fixin's, darlin'? I could roll one while you're ministering."

Lorna pauses and stares at him. Then pointedly tosses her scissors and gauze down and with a snort of disapproval disappears into the inner office.

By the time she returns from the office, he has pulled off his coat and tie. She plunks down a bottle of rye and two shot glasses on the desk and sets a cigar box on his lap. She pours two drinks and watches him fumble painfully with the rolling papers. She downs her drink and takes the box from him and hands him his drink. Then she sits on the corner of the desk and begins to roll a smoke for him.

"It's been a long, dry spell. Doesn't seem natural considering there's a deadly sin for every day of the week. The world didn't change, it's you."

"You too, huh?" he scowls as he reaches to pour another drink. She slaps his hand away,"Medicinal purposes only."

"Let's see your shingle", he reaches for and grabs the bottle this time and pours another two fingers and downs it. Lorna looks on with mild disapproval. She finishes the twist, places it in his accepting lips, strikes the Ronco lighter and fires up the gasper. She gives him time to take a few drags, then,"OK, soldier, report."

"I was on my way back to my place when one or more gorillas decided my impersonation of the firm's senior partner was very much to their liking and showed their appreciation," he winces as she returns to patching his wound.

"So, the working explanation is; they thought you were Walter."

"That's nothing, I thought a drain pipe was Walter."

She stops her ministrations,"What?"

"Nothing. Never mind", he waves her off. "Any sign he's been here since we left?" She looks around,"No. I didn't know to look in your office. He must be in pretty deep if it's come to this." She finishes with the last bandage,"You should get Doc Larson to check that first thing tomorrow."

"And who knows how much further down after tonight. Thanks," he offers as he reaches gingerly up to check her handiwork. "So, you really haven't had a chance to..." she probes.

"Sorry", Brick replies as he drapes his tie around his neck and slips on his jacket. She rises and starts to clean up,"Of course not. Let's get a cab together. I want to make sure you get home, OK. It's very late."

He washes out the glasses in the bathroom sink and returns them along with the bottle and cigar box to his office. By the time he is done Lorna awaits him at the front door. "I buzzed Joel and had him call a cab. They should be here any second." She folds her collar up around her neck and crosses out as he closes and locks the door behind them.

Outside, they settle into the taxicab as the nightwatchman closes the door for them and waves as they pull away. None of them notice the almost conical shadow that slowly crosses out to the curb to watch the vehicle's tail lights retreat. Then slowly, it shuffles across the street and into Trinity Place.

Outside Brick's apartment, Lorna follows him out of the taxicab. As they stand there, Brick starts to say goodnight, when Lorna grabs his lapels and pulls down hard, snatches the hat off of his head and probes briefly his wound one more time by street light. "Hey, I'm fine, I got a great field surgeon. Dismissed!" He grabs his hat back, but she plants a kiss on his cheek before he can pull away.

"Try to get some rest. And…. thanks," she folds herself into the taxicab and gives the cabbie her address as she pulls the door closed. Brick watches them go for a few seconds, then turns and treads heavily up the stairs and in through the orange/red front door. Once inside, now in his undershirt and trousers he pours himself three shots of vodka and falls asleep in the arm chair near his bed.

A telephone-bell rings. After the third ring, fingers fumble on wood and Brick manages to drop the phone into his lap as he brings the receiver to his ear. His responses are curt,"Hello…. Yes, speaking…. Dead? What? How can – yes…." he squints at the tinny alarm clock perched on his copy of Duke's *Celebrated Criminal Cases of America* on the side table: it reads ten minutes to four. "Give me twenty minutes,"he groans into the phone before he hangs up.

He rises and switches the lamp off and flicks on the overhead light fixture: a white frosted bowl hanging from three golden chains from the ceiling. He shuffles to the bathroom, drinks a full glass of water and fills the sink. When finished he ducks his head under the water, holding it there for several seconds before he comes up for air and towels off.

He changes his clothes, putting on a thin, white union suit, gray socks, trousers and a light- blue-striped shirt. He picks up the telephone, calls Graystone 4500 and orders a taxicab as he puts on his shoes. By the time he has his tie tied, loose tweed overcoat and hat on, the street-door-bell rings. Stuffing, keys, wallet and tobacco into his pockets he steps out into the chill, steamy morning.

The fog was thin, but the cold air still penetrated and cast burnished halos around every light source. As Brick approached the tunnel overpass he could spy a few rubberneckers even at this dull, early hour. Brick dismissed the taxicab and approached a uniformed policeman chewing gum as he leans on the parapet that overlooks Stockton Street. Brick starts to head towards the west stairs, but the officer lurches to his feet and arm bars Brick from the passage,"What do you want here?"

"Lloyd Brick. Tom Bond called me."

The patrolman squints at Brick, then,"Oh, sure you are. Didn't recognize you at first. They're down there," he waves his arm in the general direction of the tunnel mouth below them. Brick starts for the stairs, but the officer stays him again,"Better use the other stairs", he nods to the railing behind them. "Bad business."

"Bad enough", Brick replies as he turns and starts for the east stairwell entrance. After a few steps he crosses to the parapet and looks over the concrete balustrade. A car swooshes out of the tunnel and throws a glare over a small swarm of men around the bottom of the west stairwell casting their shadows into looming behemoths. Luminous ellipses bob about from electric-torch beams on the sidewall.

Brick pulls back and lopes down the stairs. At the bottom he passes a parked ambulance. It is dark with the lack of urgency. As he crosses the lane the shafts of light from several electric-torches converge on him and stop him, blindingly in his tracks. He holds up a hand to shield his eyes when a familiar voice rings out,"It's OK, boys. I called him."

Out of the glare looms a back-lit bulk,"Hello, Lloyd,"the figure hails. As he comes closer, Brick can make out the unshaven jowls, high, broad forehead, and lumbering frame of the police sergeant. The other officers nod and wave at Brick as the two men came together next to the Tuscan columns that form the arch for the stair exit to Sutter Street.

"I figured you would want to see everything before we took him away." Brick nods, but goes no further,"What've you got?"

"Got him in the back – with this." He removes a heavy pistol from his pocket and holds it out for Brick to examine. Brick leans in, but doesn't touch it,"Hm. A Webley, thirty-two caliber. Don't make 'em anymore. How many gone out of it?"

"Four pills; all of 'em in Walt. Ever seen this before?"

Brick frowns and shakes his head,'No'. Then he brushes past the sergeant and crosses to the bottom of the stairwell. A patrolman stands over a crumpled figure. That was one coat he was never going to see again. Bond comes up and plants himself behind Brick's right shoulder. "Who found him?" Brick asks stolidly.

"Man on the beat," comes the reply. "He didn't see anyone, coming or going."

"Somebody must've heard the shots."

"Somebody", Bond nodded. "We're just about to canvas the neighborhood."

"Do we actually know if he was shot here or…," he trails off with a vague gesture.

"Doesn't look like he was moved", Bond shakes his head. "His gun was tucked away, it hadn't been fired. His overcoat was buttoned; blasts burnt the fabric. By the way, the coat and hat belong to you according to the writing on the labels. Sorry, we'll have to keep them as evidence for now."

"Sure," Brick nods at Bond, then at the body,"It was in the way of a favor."

Bond looks puzzled,"Huh. Well, he had almost two hundred dollars in his wallet. Was he on the job, Lloyd?"

Brick remains staring at the stairwell. He only nods in response. "On what?" Bond presses.

"He was supposed to be tailing a fellow named Louis Pines," comes the laconic response.

"What for?"

Brick turns around and directs a blase` gaze at the sergeant,"We don't know what his game was, exactly. We were trying to find out where he lives." He smiles tightly and squeezes Bond's shoulder,"Don't crowd me, Tom." He thrusts his hands into his pockets and sighs heavily,"Guess I'm gonna hafta break the news to Walt's wife."

Bond opens his mouth as if to retort, but thinks better of it. He gestures towards the stairwell,"Want to see him, before…." he gestures diffidently towards the ambulance. But, Brick is already on his way. He cocks his head over his shoulder,"No. You're a trained detective; you've seen everything, I could."

Bond starts at this. He stares hard at Brick, but only licks his lips and catches up to Brick and says in a hoarse whisper,"Walt had the kind of reputation that ruffles a lot of feathers. This may take a while to crack."

Brick nods,"Probably,"in an absent fashion as he stares at the black and white neon 'Quiet Through Tunnel' sign. "That's not going to make city hall very happy", he says as he moves off.

Bond stops at the curb and watches as Brick makes his way through the arch at the opposite stairwell. The Alcatraz foghorn's bawl in the distance echoes down through the stairs with a mournfulness Brick does not feel.

Outside Sherry's Liquors on Nob Hill he stops at a pay phone. "Sorry to intrude on your beauty sleep more than once an evening, but there have been major developments," he said a little while after giving the number,"Walt's been shot…. Yes, he's dead…. Ah, that's the old military bearing…. Listen, you break it to Ava, I've got to – No, the hell I will. OK, thanks – and let's keep her away from the office…. I'll have enough on my hands without her hysterics…. Yes, that's it… Swell, you're an angel, 'bye'.

The fog was thinning and dawn was just limning the corner of Hyde and Post when Lloyd enters his apartment. He peels off his overcoat and jacket and tosses them on the armchair he occupied earlier. Relieving himself of his tie and collar he reflexively reaches for the vodka bottle. He pauses for a moment, then decides to make coffee instead. He rolls three cigarettes while the coffee brews, then before he settles down he decides a splash of brandy would be a bracer along with the coffee.

"It looks like long days ahead," he thinks to himself as he sits with coffee cup in one hand and cigarette in the other. Had his partner really tried to warn him of their alluring client? Is that what precipitated four slugs on the stairs? Had he even really seen him? Maybe it was his wound; he did receive a nasty crack on the head. Brick dismisses this idea almost immediately. Not because it wasn't plausible, but with everything had had now to take on, it wasn't practical. "Tom was right about Walt, though", he muses. His ex-partner's practices had earned him plenty of enmity in the city by the bay.

He was on his third cigarette when the street-doorbell rang. "Damn", he thinks. "My dance card is already full." As he reaches the front door he can hear the shuffling of large feet and some deep murmuring. He brightens immediately, "This might actually save me some shoe leather," he speculates and jerks the door open with a jovial welcome,"Hello, Tom," he said to the tall detective he spoke to at the crime scene, and "Hello, Lieutenant," to the broad man beside the police sergeant. "Come in."

Both men fix their eyes straight ahead, nod and enter in unison. Brick seats them. A pause ensues as Tom ducks his head and stares at the floor. The Lieutenant looks from Lloyd to Tom who reluctantly addresses Brick,"Did you tell Walt's wife, Lloyd?"

"How'd she take it?" the Lieutenant interjects before he can answer.

"I don't know. I don't claim to know anything about women".

The Lieutenant snorts derisively and leans forward,"How about this then, what kind of gun do you carry?"

"I don't. I don't really care for them. But, there are some at the office, of course."

"What about here?"

"No."

"Sure about that?"

Brick shrugs,"Turn the dump upside down if you want. I won't squawk – if you've got a search warrant."

Tom winces and looks askance at the floor,"Ah, Lloyd, don't be like that. You know we got our job to do and your stonewalling is no way to treat us, it ain't right."

Brick's demeanor went from self-possessed to caustic,"I don't like this. What're you birds suckin' around here for? Either tell me, or fade so I can get some shuteye."

"Who is Louis Pines?" the Lieutenant leans forward, eyes boring into Brick.

"That's who Walt was tailing."

"You already told that to Tom. What else?", the Lieutenant snaps.

"You know I can't reveal more without first discussing it with my client."

"Who's the client? You can tell us or you'll tell it in court. We're talking cold-blooded murder here."

Brick leans forward and jerks a thumb at Tom, but addresses the Lieutenant,"Ask your partner here if I'm likely to roll over on a client just because some flatfoot doesn't care for someone else's rights."

Tom groans,"Be reasonable, Lloyd. How can we turn up anything on Walt's murder if you don't share with us what you got?"

Brick leans back in his seat and intones solemnly,"I'll clean my own house."

"Uh, huh. I thought that was a distinct possibility. Didn't I, Tom?"

Tom refuses to make eye contact but grunts in what may be assent. The Lieutenant is leaning forward again, this time with a keen gleam in his eyes,"I said to Tom here: I'll bet that Brick guy is exactly the kind to keep things in the family."

Brick looks at the sergeant who still won't meet his eye,"Just where does he think this is going?"

"Well, how's this for suspicious; Tom tells me you couldn't even be bothered to take a look at your partner yourself."

Bond flushes,"Well, damn it, Lloyd you did just take off; couldn't have been there more than five minutes."

"And you didn't call Diamond's wife, we found out that you had your secretary do it," the Lieutenant jabs two thick fingers at Brick. "The coroner pegs time of death around eight to ten o'clock. Where were you then?"

"Lying like a derelict in a storefront with my head caved in," Brick thought. "And if that's true, how could Walt have been there?", was the next idea that rang in his skull. He assumes an unconcerned air, "Had some dinner at John's Grill, then walked the neighborhood thinking things over."

"About what?" the Lieutenant.

"My own private thoughts are just that, private. And no, I doubt anyone saw me. Well, I know where I stand now." He gets up and collects his tobacco pouch and papers and begins to roll a cigarette.

"The fact that he was wearing my coat and hat might seem to indicate that someone hit the wrong target."

"Sure," the Lieutenant nods. "There's that angle. Which should make you even more eager to co-operate with us. Either way, you can't buck us forever, so why not save yourself some grief and everyone else some time."

"So, your not ready to pinch me yet, are you, Maclane?" he asks the Lieutenant. Bond looks up with a worried expression, the Lieutenant only stares hard at Brick.

"I'll take that as a 'no'," he licks the flap of his twist."Then there's no reason for me to care what you think, is there?"

The Lieutenant's normally thick red neck was blossoming into violet territory as Bond placates Brick again,"Aw, be reasonable, Lloyd. You know we gotta follow up all leads."

"And this is the bright idea that brought you to my door at this uncivilized hour: I killed my partner or set him up because…?" He lights his cigarette, waves out the match and stares expectantly at this guests through the smoke that ebbs slowly through the early morning light.

The Lieutenant's jaw juts out to a pugnacious angle,"It's no secret Diamond had become a drug on business. Word on the street has him into Lima alone for almost three yards and there's the DA's office grapevine getting juicy with talk of inquest."

"He also had ten thousand in life insurance and a wife who didn't like him," Brick retorts as he picks tobacco flakes from his lower lip.

"Aw, Lloyd, that's – that's just a -", Bond murmurs, shaking his head. Brick snaps back,"Just being co-operative and providing you with leads, or isn't that what you're here for? And you just might want to speak to this Louis Pines fellow, but there I go doing you work for you -"

"Don't you worry about our procedure, Brick, just as Tom says, we're just doing our job."

"But, I do worry Lieutenant. After all, Walt learned procedure from your department and look where that's got me."

The Lieutenant launches from his chair and cocks a fist, Bond manages to barely intercede as Brick half-rises to meet the charging bull,"Aw, damn it, Lloyd, why do you gotta …. OK, OK, you two, that's enough!"

The two combatants back down, breathing heavily and locking each other in a baleful gaze.

"All right. We're done here," the Lieutenant grunts huskily."OK, Brick, we'll do our job and if you did or didn't do it, you'll get a square deal from me. For the sake of your partner. He did a lot for this city for a long time. And not everything will be forgotten."

Brick beams a cordial smile and jabs a finger at the Lieutenant,"Fair enough." He crosses to the kitchen,"How about one for the road? No hard feelings?" He returns with three glasses and pours a finger each into them from the vodka bottle. He raises his glass and the others follow.

"Success… to crime," he intones and tosses back his shot.

3

Partners

When Lloyd Brick arrives at his office at ten eighteen the next morning he'd had a little over two hours sleep, but managed to get a quick shave and hot towel and is feeling fairly braced until he sees his secretary's face. Her pallor is dull under her freckles and under her raw looking eyes there are puffy bags. She cautiously places the letters and the opener she is using down on the desk top and says in a whisper,"She's in there."

Brick winces and whispers back,"You couldn't convince her to 'amscray' for the day?

Lorna looks back at him with half-closed eyes,"After the thirty-six hours we've been through and three hours of the grieving widow, I'm feeling a little short on moxie this morning."

Brick crosses behind her and reaches under her blond locks and begins to massage her neck,"Sorry angel, you're right it's been a rough ride for -" He breaks off as the door to the inner office opens."Hello, Ava," he says to the somberly dressed woman who appears in the doorway.

"Lloyd." The word expels from her with a little too much emphasis. One gloved hand on the door frame, the other on the knob, she perches in the doorway as if expecting flight. Brick squeezes his secretary's shoulders and disengages himself. As he comes around the desk, his late partner's wife subsides back into the office.

Brick enters and closes the door behind him. They stand about five feet apart, a strained silence between them. Brick takes her appearance in: her well-turned body is wound in a long-sleeved black dress with a gold and coral inlay along the shoulders and neck. Her black hat has an embroidered veil with an edged trimmed in gold. She clenches a matching black and gold clutch tensely in front of her. Then, she launches her self at Brick and throws her arms around him,"Oh Lloyd. Isn't it just too awful?"

Brick is taken aback at first, then he reaches around and pats her consolingly on the back,"Yes, awful...." He takes advantage of their position to check the time on his wrist-watch, then slowly disentangles her and leads her to a chair in front of his desk. She seems slightly confused by the maneuver, but sits and pulls a small handkerchief from her purse and lifts her veil to apply it to her sniffling nose.

Brick is immediately flooded with an image from the day before of the mysterious Miss Daeva. A vibrant image of her cimmerian eyes appears before him. The image comes to him in extreme close-up as if he were recalling an image from a dream. When did this reverie occur?

Ava drops her hand and lifts her pale, tear-stained face and asks in a fretful tone,"Lloyd... you didn't do this, did you?"

Brick feels his eyes pop open and his jaw sag. He blinks for a moment, then explodes with a single barking laugh,"Ha!" He smacks his right first into his left palm, steps over to the front of his desk and half-sits on the edge. He folds his arms and stares at her, a wicked smile etching his face that makes his eyes glitter.

"Now, Lloyd, be nice...." She squirms in her seat and raises the small linen to her face again, her eyes still spilling anguish, but no longer meeting his own.

"You killed my husband, Lloyd, be kind to me," he sneers.

She flares at this and rises from the chair indignantly,"I saw the way you looked at me earlier. You can't say that we haven't had something between us before -"

"Some drunken fumbling at a holiday party in the past is no indication of any kind of-"

"Oh, how like a man, how like my husband!", she snaps."You get what you want and then just feel you can -"

"I don't recall our feelings ever being overwhelmingly mutual," Brick says evenly and crosses his arms even tighter across his chest. She stares at him, her hands now at her sides, fists working in frustration.

Finally,"Fine!" She yelps and turns and crosses to the door. She stops as she grasps the doorknob,"I don't suppose you know why the police would want to question me regarding Walt's life insurance, would you?"

Brick lifts his head slightly, but remains silent. Ava gives him a wry smile,"We both know Walt's habits would come home to roost one day. We've both turned a blind eye to too much to get here. But, you are the only one who is in a position to salvage what we have. I'll keep out of your way – for now. Be seeing you." And with that she slowly and enticingly turns and exits the office.

Brick uncrosses his arms and runs his hand over his face and vents,"Christ!" He takes off his hat and coat and slumps into the chair behind his desk, pulls out his cigar box and places it on the desk top. He gets as far as smoothing out the rolling paper, but keeps worrying it between his fingers as he stares sullenly at his dead partner's desk.

Five minutes later there is a soft knock on the door and Lorna lets herself in. With apprehensive eyes she clasps her hands behind the bow in the back of her dress and slowly approaches his desk,"So, how did things go?"

Brick continues to stare dully at his partner's empty desk. "She thinks I shot Walt. And I've no doubt who put that bright little idea into her head."

Lorna takes the rolling paper from his nerveless fingers and begins to roll the cigarette for him."That notion couldn't have come completely from his old pals," she said with just a little pique.

"One inebriated indiscretion does not a crime of passion make," he mumbled bitterly. "I wish I'd never met her."

"Not to speak ill of the dead, but they were a couple who almost deserved each other. Not that she didn't see some suffering at his hands."

"No doubt. He showed her the back of it often enough," Brick muses, staring again at the desk opposite.

Lorna bites her lip, tilts her chin down and says in a solicitous tone,"You don't think she killed him, do you?"

Brick starts and stares at her a moment, then chuckles lightly,"Ava? Finally fed up enough to kill the Golden Goose? Not likely. She isn't likely to do much better, not now."

Lorna,"You mean at her age," she looks at him sourly. She finishes the twist, sticks it in his mouth and lights it for him. "She's still got plenty of sugar daddy bait left, believe you me. I didn't tell you that when I went to break the news to her, I did a little sleuthing myself."

"Are you telling me?" Brick looks at her alertly keeping the amused smile on his face.

"She kept me waiting at the door while she was dressing and I tried to open the bedroom door while she made coffee and it was locked. So, when I left, I asked the doorman to her building if he had seen her the previous evening and he said that she was out by seven-thirty and didn't come back until almost midnight – and she wasn't alone." She leans into him on the desk and her voice drops into a sotto voce growl.

Brick's eyes widen with surprise and appreciation,"Nice work, but you're not going to convince me yet that she had anything to do with it. Maclane's theory is much more plausible."

Lorna,"They know better than to expect you to be paralyzed with grief. But, a suspect?"

Brick,"Any potential embarrassment to the local regime would best be nipped in the bud with any and all traces swept clean. They keep the infection localized to this office and assure the public that the cancer has been eradicated from the body politic for the good of all."

Lorna flushes angrily at this,"Even if you can't fight City Hall, let's make sure that we make it as messy for them as possible."

Brick's eyebrow's shoot up, but he keeps his humor light,"That's my fight, darlin'. Haven't you got enough to worry about with Uncle Sam's Navy?"

His secretary becomes even more animated,"That's what I've been thinking – I mean, I've been thinking that with the firm short on manpower that we could just close the office and just gumshoe it. I mean, we've got more than enough on our plate, so there's no need to be here for any clients -"

Brick flips his right palm up in her direction,"Whoa! Who is *we*?"

Lorna stares back incredulously,"Why, me and you, of course."

Brick manages out of logic and politeness to close his now gaping mouth. "It makes sense", is the first thought that rings in his head. The justification follows simply: who else could he ask or trust?

He drums his fingers on the desk top for a few moments as he prioritizes assignments in his mind.

"All right, Junior G-Man I need you to find out where this Louis Pines is. Don't do anything else, just ascertain his whereabouts. Start with the hotel dicks around Union Square, then head west if nothing turns up, but be careful." He reaches into the top desk drawer and pulls out a note pad from which he tears the first page and hands it to his secretary. "Just leave the St. Mark's to me."

"Great!" Lorna exclaims as she opens the office door for him and follows to collect her own things. He is wriggling into his coat as she tries to read the notes from the Daeva meeting and gets the office ready to close,"Then what?"

"That's plenty. Oh, before you go have Walt's name taken off everything and them put Lloyd Brick on the door by today, there's an angel. I'll call you." Installing his hat on his head, he rolls out of the door. Lorna lets out a petulant sigh. Then an idea occurs to her as she reaches for the telephone that spreads an impish smile across her dappled features.

Brick strides through the long lobby of the St. Mark's Hotel and inquires at the desk for Miss Daeva. The sleek young swell behind the counter turns to assess the mail boxes then turns back with a languid,"She checked out this morning, Mr. Brick."

"I see. Ask Mr. Benny if he would step out here, please." The clerk blinks, blandly, but puts in the request over the phone as Brick turns to take in the activity in the lavender hued vestibule. In seconds a round faced man with a receding hairline approaches Brick's left shoulder,"Good morning, Mr. Brick. My sincere condolences on your partner's demise," he offered a soft, moist hand and Brick shakes it.

"Thanks. He was in here last night. Could I ask a favor of you then ask that your forget I asked?"

The manager's smile was cordial and conspiratorial, "Certainly, come to my office, please."

He gestures the way and Brick follows. Benny offers him a seat in front of his desk, "Ferguson was on duty last night. Should I call him?"

"Not necessary. I need what ever you have on an ex-guest by the name of Karina Daeva on the QT."

"I'll be right back. Can I get you anything else while you're waiting?"

"No, thanks."

The manager nods and leaves. Brick, slowly scans the nicely appointed office with it's plush furnishings and touches of the cosmopolitan, such as the music stand and violin in the far corner. All the while taking the time to ponder getting started on his secretary's case. Even with his own head in the noose, he couldn't take a powder on a client no matter the relationship. And in this case, he was certainly bound because of the extenuating circumstances in employing his secretary in activities certainly not covered in her job description.

Mr. Benny returned mere minutes later, "She arrived last Tuesday, registering from New York. Suitcases only, no phone calls, little mail. The only time she was observed in anyone's company was a couple of days ago, speaking with a tall, dark gentleman. She went out at half past nine this morning, returned an hour later, paid her bill and had her bags taken out to a Nash touring car. Most likely a hired one according to the bellhop that assisted her. She left her forwarding address as, The Ambassador, Los Angeles."

Brick rises and thanks the manager and is led out of the office. "There's no need to get the house mixed up in anything," Brick assures the manager at the front exit. "Your discretion is appreciated, as always, Mr. Brick." They shake hands and part. Brick moves to the desk and gestures for a phone and once he has given the number, he leans on the counter and takes in the passing assemblage. When the other party picks up he says into the phone,"Hello, Frank. This is Lloyd Brick…. Can you let me have a car with a driver who can keep his mouth shut for a short trip down the peninsula? Couple hours at most…. Great, call me at the office in an hour." He hangs up, pushes the phone away, turns his collar up and heads for the door.

When Brick returns to his office he is stopped dead in his tracks by the new sign-age on the door: Lloyd Brick & Associates. He opens the door with some uncertainty. His secretary is on the phone and gestures for him to enter as she cradles the hand-piece to her ear with one hand and writes with the other,"Uh, huh…. And no forwarding address…. No, thanks anyway." She hangs up, and speaks without looking up as she finishes writing,"The Herbert Hotel. The house dick just came on duty. No one under the name of Louis Pines, but they did have a client who fits the description to a tee under the name of B. Pines. Checked out early this morning, according to the doorman, he gave the cabbie an address in Chinatown."

Brick has pulled up a chair during the proceeding and straddles it backwards as he chirps,"Thanks – associate." Lorna looks up brightly,"Your welcome. Gives the firm a sense of – means, don't you think?"

"As long as we're not actually expanding the payroll. I'm expecting a call about following up on your jar of guts, but first I need to track down our -"

His secretary flips a sheet of paper to him which, after a moment, he plucks from her,"She's at the Palace Hotel. You're to ask for Miss Manes."

Just then the telephone rings and Lorna snatches up the handset,"Lloyd Brick and associates," she says vividly. Brick has the urge to correct her, but glances at the door and relents. "It's Frank about the car," she says, leaning on the desk with both elbows and covering the mouthpiece. "He says he can have a driver here by four if that suits." Brick nods in acquiescence and she relays his affirmation through the phone, hangs up and looks at him expectantly.

"So, is it hard to gumshoe it in heels?"He smiles, teasingly. His secretary looks back at him in all seriousness,"Not with the modern telephone. I know many of the ladies at the hotel switchboards and so it was more a matter of nails than heels," she iterates this by circling her index finger in the air. Brick feels a bit discomfited by the apparent ease with which the information was obtained, but nods in appreciation,"Outstanding. Let's see," he consults his watch,"I'm off to play the Palace."

"Anything else, I can take care of, while you're being seduced?", she says with a completely sincere expression. "No, but I can hardly wait to see the new letterhead," he replies as he backs out of the office door with a tip of his hat.

4

In the Air

L loyd Brick strides up the steps and under the middle awning of the Palace Hotel and once inside moves left through the white arches etched in gold to the reception desk and asks for "Miss Manes." The stern, monocled clerk nods and consults the telephone and after a few moments he reveals that she is waiting for him at the pool. Brick thanks him and heads for the elevators.

When Brick enters the pool area it appears to be deserted except for the shreds of vapor lifting off of the pool's blue surface under the atrium roof. The marine layer has burned off and the sun now stands out in glaring contrast. Not catching sight of her immediately, he starts to walk towards the other end of the pool when -

There she is.

Slowly emerging from around one of the tiled pillars. She is wearing white, broad-rimmed sunglasses encrusted with rhinestones. More significantly, she sports a tropical patterned bikini with a ruched halter top and is perched on top of matching color blocked, deco peep-toed pumps. Lloyd can almost feel the whisper of her well-turned thighs as she stops and cocks one knee in front of the other.

She slips her shades down and even from this distance her eyes glint as if bouncing across the water in a green flash through the mist rising from the heated pool. She slides her eye-wear up to the top of her head and extends her hand in invitation to join her at the blue striped chaise lounges near the opposite end of the pool. This dank time of year provides them with virtual privacy even in this public space.

Brick seats himself on the lower portion of the neighboring chaise, while his client also does the same. She clasps her hands between her knees and looks demurely at Brick,"Mr. Brick, I've a terrible confession to make." She looks up, her mouth down-turned in affliction,"That story about a sister was just that – a story. Can you forgive me?" Her eyes well; irises dark, shimmering pools.

"Oh, that," Brick gestures breezily,"we didn't need to believe your story as much as we needed to believe in your two hundred dollars."

"I see," she deflates and bites her lower lip."Still, am I to blame in any way for – for what happened yesterday?"

"You lied to us about your sister, but as I said, that doesn't count, Miss… Which is it? Daeva or Manes?"

She blushes now and her eyes roll away from him,"Neither. Actually it is Markov, Darya."

"Well, Dzyevooshka Markov, Darya, you warned us that Pines was violent, the situation volatile, we take certain risks in our business. Walt knew that. So, no. No, I wouldn't say you were to blame." She starts at first when she hears him pronounce Russian, but droops again when he absolves her.

"Unless, there's more to your story that you have yet to reveal." He says pointedly, but she remains distracted,"But, I'll always blame myself."

"There'll be plenty of time for guilt later, if you feel you must indulge, but in the meantime, there are a flock of detectives, assistant D.A.'s and the press hot on the trail of murder and maybe more. What do you want to do?"

"They don't know about me, do they?" She rocks back and her hands rise to her collarbone.

"Not yet, I needed to talk to you first."

She casts her gaze down. Under thick lashes her eyes flicker with distress,"And if they did know, the story I presented would make me another suspect in their eyes, wouldn't it?" She looks up pleadingly.

Brick nods,"Not that my late partner didn't engender plenty of other candidates. But, they know he was on the job and we have to tell them something. This Louis Pines, for instance. What was the upshot of your evening? Is he behind all this?"

She leans forward and places a hand on his knee,"Yes, I lied. And I would only continue to do so if I didn't admit that I have been making a career of it for so long that I...," She sighs heavily."I've been bad, maybe even worse than you could know. But, I am all alone now and I don't know...." She seems overwhelmed again and he eyes begin to well and wander."I know I've no right to ask you to trust me, but.... I do so desperately need your help. And I will tell you what it's all about, but not now, I can't now, but please trust me that I will when I can. Please trust me that far, Mr. Brick. You're resourceful, brave, strong. Surely, you can spare some of these exceptional qualities. You wouldn't begrudge them to someone truly in need."

Her tenebrous eyes are now riveted on him and a sudden vertiginous effect claims him: a sudden flush over his body and his pores open like spillways; rivulets under his arms and over his brow. It feels as if the sun is being focused through the atrium ceiling like a magnifying glass trained on the back of his head. He stands, woozily and peels off his coat, jacket and hat,"Excuse me...." Her hand slides away and she watches as he turns away from her and tugs at his tie and collar.

"Oh, you've been hurt!" She exclaims as she spies the small bandaged portion of his skull. "Please...." She pulls a small handkerchief from the lounge, rises, reaches up and grasps his shoulders and guides him back down. His knees are too weak to resist. "Too easy, too easy", he tries to warn himself in his head, but strength seems just out of his grasp. Is it his old wound exacerbated by last night's assault?

Once she has him seated she helps loosen his collar and tie," I know it's an impossible thing to ask, especially in light of your partner's death, but I beg you on my knees to trust to give me a little more time and I will requite it, I swear. I have nowhere else to turn. You can help me, Mr. Brick. Please. Be generous, Mr. Brick." Her voice seeps like smoke into the chambered nautilus of his brain.

She mops his clammy brow,"Look at me, Mr. Brick." He turns his bemused face to her. All at once his vision is filled with her eyes; dark gleams in ambush. They shimmer with an amorphous essence and seem to exude an incessant whispering that fills his mind with desperate entreaties. He grabs the fragrant linen from her hand and finishes wiping his face.

Taking a deep breath his slowly stands and faces her,"You shouldn't need much of anyone's help; you're good, you're awful good. It's chiefly your eyes and that flutter you get in your voice when you say things like 'Be generous, Mr. Brick.'"

She looks up at him in genuine shock, her mouth agape, eyes vast with disbelief. Then she flushes and drops her gaze," I guess I deserved that. But I do so need your help, that much is the distressing truth no matter what fiction I couch it in. I'm the only one to blame that you can't believe me now."

Brick's eyes flicker and he his upper lip peels back for a moment in a grimace,"Now you are dangerous," he hisses. She holds up his hat to him, tremulously but cannot meet his gaze. Brick stares at the hat. Then,"What happened last night?"

"Pines came to the hotel a little after eight, as he said, and I met him in the lobby as requested. Mr. Diamond had already been there for a good twenty minutes. I suggested we go for a walk to talk and we headed down toward Market Street." She tucks the hat into her lap."But, I'm afraid we did not get very far."

"Oh?" Brick lowers himself into the lounge, she shifts her legs, feet on the tile, offering him her back-lit profile. "He said he came alone, because she didn't want to see me – which I refuse to believe – and that the family should just leave them alone as they were happy and had plans to go way far away together."

"And was my partner on the scene?"

"Yes. I tried, begged, pleaded with that man to at least take me to my sister one more time before – but, he became violent and even threatened to – to strike me if I didn't let go of him. He only relented when he realized what a scene we were making there on the street."

"And then?"

She shakes her head, her hair rippling with sunshine,"He stalked away. So fast. Down the street. That was the last I saw of him. And your partner, he winked at me and I saw him follow Pines at a distance, although I think he was so angry he would never have noticed Mr. Diamond any way."

"Which way? Down Market?"

She nods."Then you wouldn't have any idea why they would be at Bush and Stockton, where Walt was found?" He asks. She shakes her head again,"No. Would that not be near where Mr. Pines was staying?"

"A bit out off the beaten path," Brick muses. "Then what did you do after they had gone?" In spite of the need for the interrogation, Brick found his gaze lingering on the opulent consonance between her skin and hair.

"I went back to the hotel and to bed, though I slept very little. Then when I went out for breakfast this morning I saw the early editions and read about – about Mr. Diamond. After that I hired a car and picked my luggage up from the hotel. I knew I would have to move right away after I'd found my room had been searched."

"You're room at the St. Mark's was searched?"

"Yes, while I was at your office."

"Hopefully you haven't been followed here," he ruminates. "So, there are things you can't- won't tell me." She drops her head and nods, ashamed. "If I'm going to help you – if," he waves a finger in her now expectant face,"I need some kind of line on this Louis Pines."

She sets her elbows on her thighs and steeples her hands in front of her piquant mouth," I don't know really. He just showed up outside the hotel one evening and I realized he was following me. The following evening he did the same and I confronted him," he fingers fold together,"at first I thought he might kill me, but after a while I was able to convince him that I could be more useful as an ally."

"In what enterprise?"

She bites the knuckle on her index finger and doesn't reply.

"I see. And you wanted him shadowed because?"

She lowers her hands and examines her cuticles in a minute fashion,"He told me that he would have to take my offer to his 'boss'. I needed to know who that was at the very least,"then she crumples her fists to her breasts,"but mostly, I was just afraid. Afraid of him, his vicious attitude, I couldn't be sure if he even had a boss or if he was just tormenting me."

"You keep referring to him as dangerous. How dangerous? Enough to put four pills into some poor unsuspecting slob's back?"

Karina gasps and clutches her throat,"Is that what happened to poor Mr. Diamond? How horrible! But, yes, Louis Pines was definitely armed, he showed me a pistol when he threatened to kill me."

"So, you're involved in a mysterious activity with violent and possibly deadly cohorts and I have a dead partner who may or may not have been a victim of your need for a background check-slash-bodyguard." He stands and paces a short distance, worrying his right ear with his fingers, his right elbow resting on his left hand, slung across his waist. He turns around, crosses back and looks down at Karina who returns his gaze with a pale, but expectant air.

"Until I can ascertain your role in what happened to my partner last night, I don't know that I can help you much. I may just have to tell the police what I know and you'll have to take your chances." Her whole being seems to diminish except for her eyes which expand with desperation. She chokes out,"You – wouldn't go to the police?"

"Go?" he roars,"how can I miss them? They never leave. All I have to do is stand still and they'll swarm me like army ants." He waves his arms and his voice echoes off of the tiles.

Her head drops and her hand raises tremulously with his hat in it,"I-I understand. You can't be expected to risk so much for a total stranger. I thank you for what you've done, but it's hopeless, I suppose."

Brick vacillates, then growls in frustration and all but snatches his hat from her and asks,"How much money have you got?" The question startles her; she looks up and stammers,"I- I don't…. maybe five hundred dollars or so-"

"Can you raise any more?" he places his hat on his head and picks up his coat and jacket and slings them over his forearm.

"Um, I suppose I could. I have some jewelry."

"You'll have to hock them. Try at Mission and Fifth; they're the best."

"Well, I'll have to retrieve them from my room and -" as she starts to rise from the chaise, he takes her hand. A voltaic charge leaps from her fingers to his. They both grasp each others hand a little tighter and their eyes flicker in unison.

"Thank you," she murmurs, her face turned up to his. "I'll be back as soon as I can with the best news I can manage," he replies as he escorts her to the pool exit.

When Brick returns to his office at a quarter to four, his secretary and erstwhile partner is just again hanging up the telephone. "What's stirring?", he inquires.

"I just got off the phone with my cousin, he wants to meet with you tomorrow."

He claps his hands and rubs them together as his eyes squint into the future,"For a while I've had the feeling that if Walt were to disappear from the picture that things could only look up. Oh, by the way, did you remember to send flowers?"

"I did. Something a woman would always think of," she replies, preening a little.

"Indeed and speaking of female attributes, what does your woman's intuition tell you about Miss Daeva?"

There is a sharp intake of breath and she presses her lips together. Then her brows contract as she looks at Brick," I suppose I should show more solidarity with a fellow female, but...." her eyes shift down in contemplation. Brick flushes and scowls with concern,"But, what?"

"It's just that – I'm not saying she's bad necessarily, it's just that...." her eyes rove around the ceiling for a moment, then,"She has this queer affect, I mean, she seems like the type of person who gets their way more often than not and that can make trouble – for everyone." She winces and looks at Brick apologetically.

Brick muses,"She has shown a tenuous relationship with the truth. Oh, and case in point; her name's Markov." But then he brightens and taps the tip of Lorna's nose with his index finger, jovially,"Anyway she's forked over seven hundred clams in two days. There's hope for that paycheck yet, partner."

His secretary looks back at him earnestly,"As long as no one, including the client ends up paying too much in the end."

Brick opens his mouth to respond, but just then the telephone rings and Lorna answers it,"Lloyd Brick and Associates. Oh, thanks, Joel." She replaces the handset in the cradle and looks up at him,"Your ride is here."

"Then it's a good thing I never sat down," Brick answers and tips his hat in salute as he backs out. "Close up shop for today, angel. You've had a full day."

A little under an hour later, Brick is craning his neck out of the back window of a Dodge Luxury Liner at the intersection of Crisp and Griffith Streets. A chain-link fence topped with barbed-wire stretches across the street. A new sentry box striped yellow and black was set back behind a gate. He scowls at the impasse and was mentally searching his memory for an old shipmate who might afford him access when the driver spoke up,"They expanded several blocks inland this year. I hear it's cuz of this new hush-hush department they got."

Brick merely nodded. This would jive with what he was vaguely aware of in the deep Pacific Ocean regarding naval experiments with the new nuclear age. Feeling he has wasted the afternoon he is about to order the driver back, when a Chevrolet C-10 stake bed truck rolls up to the gate. A sentry opens the gate for the vehicle and it is waved through back out onto the civilian streets. As the truck rumbles by, Brick catches site of the driver and exclaims,"Well, I'll be a – Driver, follow that truck!"

"Yes, sir!" The ruddy faced youth behind the wheel enthuses. He spins around on the shoulder of the road, kicking dust and gravel into the air. After about twenty seconds he is directly behind the truck and Brick orders him,"Get him to pull over." The driver merely nods with a smirk and drops the car into passing gear and roars ahead of the lumbering navy blue flatbed. He honks his horn and deliberately slows down until the truck squeals to a halt.

Brick is out of the sedan almost before it stops. As he approaches the truck cab, he can hear the driver swearing,"What the hell is this? Some goddamn hijacking or what the -" he breaks off as Brick thumps the hood of the lend lease conveyance on his way to the driver's side door. "Avast there, helmsman," Brick calls out as he hops up on the running board under the driver's door. The two men clasp forearms.

Ten minutes later, he waves goodbye to the leather-colored old salt behind the wheel of the land cruiser and hops back into the sedan and instructs the driver to return to the office. He reviews the information on the way: a new branch of the Navy called the Naval Radiological Defense Laboratory now held sway over the base. They were examining target vessels from nuclear experiments in the Bikini Islands. His old shipmate had just finished delivering a truckload of geese and told of other animals like goats and pigs being trucked in. When Brick asked him what happened once his charges were delivered he looked away for a few moments and then said, he had no idea, but he'd heard that everyone on the base was promised a ham for the holidays.

Arriving back at his office, he is surprised to see lights still on inside. He opens the door and finds Lorna dressed to leave, sitting behind her desk. She looks up at him expectantly.

"You realize that partner status doesn't qualify you for overtime." Her eager expression falls,"What should I tell my cousin?"

"Tell him we're still on for tomorrow. When and where?"

"At the amphibious base across the bay. He has a detail there. He says to take the frontage road to Fleming Point and he'll meet you there at ten. The security there is fairly lax, so he feels pretty comfortable there."

Brick nods and heads for his office,"Just let me get a couple things." He enters his office and closes the door. He pauses to take in Diamonds empty desk, then decides to rifle it quickly for clues. He quickly, but quietly scrutinizes every drawer. He finds one of the office hand guns, loaded. He replaces it making a mental note to return it to the safe when he has more time. The only object that sparks a notion is a red and black matchbook advertising D.W. Low's Club Shanghai on Grant Avenue. He taps the cardboard in his hand as he recalls his secretary mentioning his partner having a rendezvous in the neighborhood.

He starts to head for the office-door when he hears the corridor-door open and close. Soft voices tickle his ears as he moves slowly towards the office door, when a soft knock sounds and Lorna cracks the door open and leans in, whispering,"Speaking of queer; I know it's late, but there's someone here to see you. He just kind of appeared out of nowhere. Should I tell him to come back tomorrow during regular business hours?"

Brick frowns in thought: he should follow up on this tenuous lead on his partner. He steps closer to the door to try to get a glimpse of the potential client when he picks up a familiar scent. Could it be the same one as he experienced after the mugging?

"No. In with him, darling," he says as he hangs up his coat and hat and settles himself in the tilting wooden chair behind his desk. Lorna holds the door open and gestures to the outer office,"Won't you please come in, Mr. Terranova?"

Brick can hear a soft shuffling of feet and the scent becomes slightly more redolent. A short, conical bulk of a being in a camel's hair coat with the collar turned up and a black, boss-of-the-plains hat with an enormous brim trundles in before him and he almost bolts upright in his chair as he seems to recognize his shadow from the previous evening. When the figure plops itself into the chair opposite Brick's desk, it's feet do not touch the floor.

Lorna's oblique gaze rests on their guest as she hovers at the door,"Um, will you gentlemen be needing anything?" Brick keeps his eyes in front of him as he waves her good night,"No, thank you, angel. Carry on, smartly. Lock the door when you go."

"Thanks, I will. I'm gonna stop off and leave a message for housekeeping. Weird thing; the ashtrays in the hall have all been spilled," and with one last skeptical glance she exits, closing the door behind her. Brick quarter turns and rests one hand on the desktop as he asks,"What is it we can do for you, Mr. Terranova?"

Brick's guest slowly casts a glance around the room, gloved hands resting on his knees, his face further obscured by eyeglasses with large, tinted frames. Only his nose – dark, pitted, furrowed – protruded to give any indication of an origin. "If he had topped the ensemble off by swathing his head in bandages," Brick thought,"the effect would have resembled Claude Rains in his most 'nothing' film role."

When his gaze returns front, Terranova responds in a gravelly voice."I thank you for agreeing to see me at such an hour. May a stranger offer condolences on your partner's unfortunate demise?" Another foreign accent, Brick thought, but as the name would seem to indicate, something Latin. He nods, in response,"Thanks."

"More than chance brings me to your establishment, this evening. I have reason to believe that an operative at your firm may have information regarding an item I have been pursuing on behalf of the object's rightful owner. I am prepared to pay up to ten thousand dollars for the return of said property to the rightful owner with – what is the phrase? - no questions asked."

"And just whom do you suppose has what you are after?" Brick asks lightly, his tone polite, but easy.

Terranova shakes his head slowly,"That is the question I intend to discover right now," and from his sleeve he extends a compact, flat, black pistol."You will please clasp your hands at the back of your head. I intend to search your offices."

5

Crackup

Brick's eyes never leave Terranova's face in spite of the gun leveled at him. A rattling sound emits from Brick's guest and he brings the back of his hand to his mouth; almost a cough of apology. He gestures with the gun,"Please to step into the center of the room where I may keep you in my line of sight. And please be assured that if you hinder me in any way, I will most certainly shoot you."

"Sure", Brick replies as he stands and pushes the chair away with his legs. He dutifully follows instructions all the while remaining placid, his face almost bored in it's calmness.   As he comes around the desk, Terranova orbits around him and trades places,"That's far enough," he growls as he plants himself behind the desk. "I shall begin here," he reaches down and pulls out the first drawer.

"Could I ask a small favor?" Brick asks congenially. Terranova stops. "The cigar box, I'd like a smoke while I'm waiting." Pause. Terranova flips open the box. Inspects it, then tosses it disdainfully on the desktop corner closest to Brick. Brick brings his hands out to the side of his head,"May I?"

Terranova nods and impatiently gestures with the gun. Brick opens the box and starts to remove the contents,"Just need these," he indicates as he takes out the rolling papers, then the tobacco pouch. Keeping the lid of the box between himself and the stranger, he quickly dumps the loose leaf tobacco into the bottom of the box, then flings it into Terranova's face.

The dry flakes erupt into a cloud as the stout figure raises his arms to fend off the projectile. Brick takes the interim to scramble behind his late partner's desk. While Terranova sputters and stomps around the desk to find him, Brick - with a small nod of thanks to his late partner's carelessness - retrieves the gun left erroneously behind from the bottom drawer. By the time his assailant is clear of his desk, Brick rises from behind the other and simply states,"Mine's bigger."

The bulky intruder wavers for a moment, then with a growl, thrusts out his weapon and fires. The report sounds like a book hitting the floor. The shot shears the sleeve of Brick's coat and shatters the window. Brick squeezes off a round - the sound is like a cannon going off in the small space - which catches Terranova in the left shoulder and sends him stumbling back into the office door. He bounces off of it and drops to his hands and knees. Brick keeps the gun leveled as he slowly advances on the prostrate figure.

The small pistol lies on the floor where it was dropped. As Brick bends down to retrieve it, Terranova rises to his knees. His left arm dangles from the shoulder. He reaches for it reflexively, then looks at it. Brick now stands with a pistol in each hand. Terranova looks up at Brick, then with his right hand he tears his left arm away and flings it, back-handed at Brick. The sleeve strikes Brick, spilling crumbling fragments of dark material across the room and sending him crashing into his desk.

As Brick struggles to his feet, he still has his own gun in his hand, and starts to look for the other, but Terranova is suddenly on him, his remaining hand clutching Brick's throat. The rotund being has prodigious strength and Brick finds himself beginning to lose consciousness. He manages to bring the gun to bear on Terranova's torso and pulls the trigger. The detonation is so close, that the sound is muffled, but the concussion knocks Terranova away. Brick staggers, choking to his feet. He makes it to the office door, opens it and stumbles into the reception area.

Reeling, he makes it to his secretary's desk and reaches for the telephone, but only succeeds in knocking it to the floor. As he drops to his hands and knees to recover it, he spies Terranova shambling out of his office towards the corridor-door. Brick can hardly believe what he is witnessing. He rises from the floor and maneuvers around the desk, pistol at the ready. Terranova seems to notice and he turns from the door. The left side of the camel hair coat is scorched and shredded. Material flaps loosely and the hillock of a figure seems to have a crescent carved out of him.

For the first time, Brick registers that the hat is gone and the eye-glass lenses are shattered, revealing black and ivory orbs, wide and glaring. The face is dusky and mapped with fissures and cracks. A cleft opens in the lower half, revealing robust, yellowed teeth in a sneering grin. He starts to amble towards Brick who backs away, stumbles over the fallen phone and inadvertently pulls the trigger.

Another deafening explosion. But, Brick can see just before he hits the floor that the shot strays wide and ruptures the glass water bottle on the office cooler. The glass and liquid flare out in Terranova's direction. The water hits him like an ocean wave and he cowers and cringes. Brick rolls up on his elbows and watches transfixed as Terra nova utters crackling whimpers,"'No, no, no…." Below him a dark, glutinous mass is puddling. His trousers and coat seemed to be deflating, but he starts to scramble once more towards Brick.

Brick scrambles to feet in a panic and lurches for the outer door, but coherent remains of Terranova latch onto him and start to drag him to the floor. Brick grabs for the doorknob, but it is too slippery to grip. He looks up in agony and spies - the transom. Grasping the doorknob as best he can and using the fallen cooler as a make-shift step, he launches himself up and with his head and shoulders thrusts the frame back, shattering the hinges. As his aggressor continues to cleave to him with astonishing adhesiveness, he pulls himself up and out the transom. He lands heavily on his shoulder in the hallway and manages to careen to the elevator just in time to collapse into the arms of the terrified night watchman.

Brick awakes in his bed in his apartment. He looks down past his feet towards the living room where there seems to be a light and soft music playing. He rolls up and sits at the edge of the bed, then rises and makes his way to the door. He stops in the doorway as he spies Darya. She is dressed in a pale green negligee and holding a tumbler with liquor up in one hand, the other holding the hem of her gown as she slowly sways to music on the radio. She softly sings along," What good is a song if the words just don't belong, And a dream must be a dream for two. No good alone, to each his own, For me there's you." With that she turns and sees him. She smiles a little sloppily and holds her arms out in invitation. He starts towards her when there is a sound outside the door. He stops. Was that a scream?

He turns and crosses to the door. In the background he can hear Darya say in a low, warning voice,"Don't open it." He pauses, his hand on the knob. Then he turns it and opens the door. As he steps into the door frame, his late partner materializes, dressed as he last saw him, in Brick's coat and hat. He rushes towards Brick, screaming. What appears to be orange and red flames seem to be emanating from his back.

Brick snaps awake and sits up, sweating and panting for breath. He is on a cot in the small office used by the house detectives and night watchmen. Lorna, looking tousled and bleary comes to him,"OK, OK, it's all right. I knew I shouldn't have left you alone with that creep." She offers him a glass of water. His shoulder curses the movement as he reaches for it, but manages to swallow most of the glasses' contents.

"What happened after I left? It looks like the OK Corral in there, except for no blood."

Brick shakes his head,"OK. So, that part wasn't a dream. I'm not sure how comforting that is," he places his hands over his face and massages around his eyes," The damned munchkin tried to hold me up in my own office. Only when he was doused with water, could I get away." He drops his hands into his lap and stares into the distance,"I mean he dissolved like Margaret Hamilton. What the hell is going on?"

Lorna seems about to speak, but hearing voices outside she leans into him and whispers,"I don't know, but I don't think I'd mention your trip to the land of Oz to the Lieutenant, Dorothy." She stands up just as the office door flings open to reveal his old pals; Maclane and Bond. The Lieutenant seems almost jovial, his partner, discomfited.

"Well, Brick, let's have a talk about your interior decorating ideas."

"Nothing to tell. My late partner forgot to do some housekeeping and I didn't know the thing was loaded."

The two policemen share a glance. Then the Lieutenant speaks up,"You really expect us to believe -"

"I don't give a tinker's cuss what you think, it was an accident."

"There are three rounds gone from your gun, I assume it's yours, the thirty-eight."Brick rubs his face and nods in assent,"I – like I said, I didn't know it was loaded. It discharged when it took it out of the drawer and, surprised, I dropped it on the desk and it went off again."

"That's two," Maclane snaps back quickly.

Brick, realizes he's caught short, then remembers the sequence of events and takes a   calculated risk and asks:"And how many slugs did you find?"

The two policemen exchange a sour glance, then Bond says,"Only two."

"Maybe the cylinder wasn't full. Like I said, I didn't have a chance to really check."

The pair exchange more incredulous glances. Tom looks sadly at Brick,"This have anything to do with Walt, Lloyd?"

"Not to my knowledge."

"What about your being found unconscious by the night watchman?"

"I wasn't unconscious, just a little…. rattled, that's all – the old wound, you know sometimes loud noises in small spaces….", he shrugs and looks away. Annoyed and embarrassed to have to resort to using his infirmity in service of such perfidy.

"Maybe we a should take this downtown. Get your hat." The Lieutenant stops smiling.

"Ah, come on, Lieutenant, there's no body. Don't you have actual murders to solve?"

"I could take you in now just for discharging a weapon inside city limits."

"And make a lot of unnecessary paperwork and heartburn for everyone? There are real criminals out there."

"I'm not so sure I'm not looking at one now," the Lieutenant scowls. "Maybe you were brushing up for your next victim."

Brick springs from the cot and cocks a fist, Lorna utters a short cry. Bond moves in between the two men again,"Hey, hey, now. None of that. Knock it off, you two!"

Both men stop straining towards each other. Tom, cocks his head towards the door,"Come on Lieutenant. We're not going to get any more out of him now."

His partner shrugs him off, his face red with exertion and emotion. "All right, Brick. Maybe you're right in buckin' us. But, you can't keep it up forever." He turns on his heel and abruptly exits the small room.

"Stop me when you can," Brick mutters as he sits again on the cot. Tom Bond looks at him with small, reproachful eyes,"I sure as hell hope you know what you're doing." He shakes his head ruefully and follows his senior partner out.

Lorna watches them go, then sidles up to Brick and whispers,"I found these scattered on the floor. He must've dropped them in the fight." She stealthily hands him three passports. Brick frowns and scans each quickly. They are from three different countries with a different picture of Terranova in each of them. They share an inquisitive glance. "Thanks", Brick says and stuffs them in his pocket.

A few hours later Brick is in his undershirt and trousers in his bathroom. The air in the room is swirling; steamy from the water vapor. He stands in front of the round mirror above the sink, shaving. He nicks himself. He winces and looks down around the wash basin for a styptic pencil when he feels someone embrace him from behind. He looks up to see -

Darya. Her face is perched over his right shoulder. She reaches up and with the middle finger of her right hand and scoops at the cut on his face. She holds the blood daubed finger up to the light. Then, with an impish look in her eye, she dips the finger in her mouth and sucks on it, giggling. Alarmed, Brick turns to confront her, but she vanishes into the mist.

Brick starts awake again. Sitting up, he rests his head in his hands for a minute, then says to himself,"OK. That's gotta stop." He slowly rises and pads into the living area and consults the alarm clock: it reads 11:49. "Damn," he thought,"slept half the day away." Flexing his sore shoulder he enters the bathroom, strips and spends the next fourteen minutes in a hot shower.

Thirty-three minutes later, freshly groomed, he is stirring sugar into his coffee with one hand, while propping a newspaper on the table with another. But, his focus is on the tall, dark stranger that ostensibly is window shopping across the street. He noticed him loitering around the corner below his building and now here he was again, across the street from Herbert's Grill, peering into a haberdashery window.

Minutes later when Brick is coming out of Marquand's 'Little Cigar Store' on the corner of Powell and O'Farrel, the statuesque figure is one of four people waiting for the cable car on the next corner. He had to meet with Darya Markov soon, so Brick decides that if tall, dark and hairy craves his company so much, that it was incumbent upon him to take this stranger on a bit of a scenic tour.

He catches a west-bound street-car, pays his seven cents and watches from his window seat as the figure lopes across the street and boards the same car at the rear. Brick smiles and slumps a bit in his seat and pulls his hat down over his eyes as if he intends to be there a while. At the corner of Hyde Street just before the street-car resumes it's route, he jumps up and exits the vehicle. He strides quickly towards the cable car that is just preparing to disembark. Once aboard he swings around to watch his latent escort grab the last bit of rail as the car lurches north.

At Lombard he casually hops off and saunters down the circuitous block, whistling all the while even as he enters his apartment on the next block down. Before he opens the door, he knows what to expect. His rooms were not nearly as disheveled as he thought they might be, but there was no mistaking the signs of a search. After satisfying himself that, indeed nothing was missing, he left the apartment, strolled east to Columbus Avenue and caught the Powell – Mason cable car south.

At the corner of Powell and Bush Streets he leisurely abandons the cable car and stopping only once in front of the Grant Hotel to make sure he hadn't lost his shadow, walks the two blocks to Grant Avenue and turns left into Chinatown. The Shanghai Club was on the left-hand side halfway down the block. He knocks on the closed door and after a minute a hostess appears in a red, sleeveless cheongsam dress. He removes his hat and asks for the manager on duty, and she leads him back through the darkened club.

She leaves him waiting outside the manager's door to announce his presence and he takes the time to scope out the checkered tablecloths, the vaulted blue ceiling with stars and yellow pagoda near the dance floor. The hostess returns, and holds the door open for him and gestures for him to enter. He steps in and she retreats and closes the door. Stepping out from behind a desk, a Chinese gentleman of middle years, graying hair, high forehead and prodigious earlobes salutes him and Brick returns the fist/palm salute and utters,"Dee-mah."

"Ho-ho", is the reply. And the two stand, smiling at each other. "Fong Wan, I didn't expect to see you here."

The older gentleman nods,"I've gone from owning an interest to owning." He picks up and holds out a red and black menu with a photograph of himself in the right top corner and the legend 'The Chinese Follies-Bergere of the America's'. And if that motto wasn't convincing enough, the prominent feature of the cover was a photograph of a scantily clad Miss Lana Wong in a strapless bikini top and black chiffon skirt.

"Herbs and entertainment, a logical match," Brick observes as he hands the menu back to the smiling proprietor. "Please sit, and tell me how I may be of service to you," Fong gestures, but Brick declines,"Thanks, but I've got someone waiting for me. I believe my partner was a habitue` recently."

Fong nods and adds,"My sympathies on his passing." Brick nods in acknowledgment as Fong retreats behind his desk and sits,"Your partner was a generous admirer of the ladies."

"No doubt," Brick agrees,"but, I'm given reason to believe he was also involved in some business in Chinatown. Business that seems to have turned fatal."

The Asian gentleman purses his lips and leans forward with his elbows on the desk,"Due to certain recent business entanglements, I am afraid I can only suggest a line of inquiry, I am sure you understand." Brick nods, signifying his satisfaction. Fong stares at him steadily and in a low tone says,"There is an individual among us, but not of us, here in Chinatown. A 'Shanghailander' who rose amongst the white Russian enclave. It is considered anathema to speak his name." And with that he reclines into his chair and sets his hands on the arm rests.

"Mm," Brick grunts in response, nodding his head. He smiles wryly,"Must've been something of significance all right." He fist-palms and says,"Mh-goy". Fong salutes back,"Juk-nay-ho-won." He presses a buzzer on his intercom and within moments the hostess is there to usher Brick out. As she closes the door behind her he gestures to the back and says,"I can see myself out. Thanks." She nods and smiles, he tips his hat and leaves.

Fifteen minutes later he is knocking on the door to Darya Markov's room at the Palace Hotel. Judging by the alacrity with which she throws open the door once she hears his voice, it seems that she might not have been certain of his return. She greets him in a negligee of chiffon and satin in coral.

He scans the sitting room's furniture and desk as she takes his hat and coat. Fresh flowers in squat, modern vases bespeckle the room with a varied and vibrant palette. "And the best news you can manage is?" She asks with a smile that is betrayed by the anxiety in her eyes.

Brick looks at her deliberately; scrutinizing her without any pretense. She blushes under his determined gaze and begins to fuss with the nearest flower arrangement. Finally, he relaxes his face into a small, but encouraging smile,"You're in the clear. The cops don't need to know about you for the foreseeable future." She takes a deep breath, holds it, then allows her face also to relax and smile albeit tremulously. She herself all but collapses with relief on the settee,"How ever did you manage it?" She gestures for him to sit by patting the space next to her.

"Sheer obstinacy at this point, but there are still things that can be begged, borrowed or stolen for the time being in San Francisco."

"And you won't get into any trouble?"

"I don't mind a certain amount of trouble; keeps me in practice." He sits opposite her in the chair facing, which causes her color to rise even more."You're not really the person you try to portray, are you? The schoolgirl manner, the damsel in distress."

She pales slightly and her mouth gapes in surprise. She quickly looks off and says faintly,"I told you I've been bad – maybe worse than you could know."

"You're right; I've heard that speech before. Now, tell me something I don't know or at least drop the helpless innocent act. We won't get anywhere with that."

She huffs out a sigh, brushes her hair back behind her ear and moisture from her eyes and turns to him,"Yes, sir." She says mockingly and holds her hand to her heart.

"I had a visit from a Senor Terranova, last night," he says as off-handedly as possible, stretching out in the chair and focusing on his feet as they extend. She freezes. Then asks in small voice,"You – you know him?"

Brick shakes his head and frowns, still not looking at her,"No. He stopped by the office. Said he had some business to discuss about the return of some property." His tone remains careless and conversational. She rises stiffly from the settee and moves to another flower arrangement and adjusts a few blooms, then she crosses to the coffee table and retrieve a cigarette from an inlaid box and lights it with the formidable chrome light next to it.

Brick watches her, the right corner of his mouth lifted in a small but appreciative grin. She then strolls to the window and flips at the curtains as if to glance at the traffic on Montgomery Street. She returns to the settee and now placidly arranges herself on the seat and asks,"And just how did you come to ask me about him?"

"You two seem to have concomitant taste in scents."

Darya's brow wrinkles in confusion. Another pause as she wipes her hands on her thighs and asks,"What did he have to say about me?"

"Nothing."

"So, your supposition about the two of us revolves around this 'scent'."

Brick turns his gaze upon her,"You gave us a phony cover story, and there are now too many threads coming together at the same time not to entertain the premise."

Darya looks at him with half-closed eyes, her chin tilted up, staring through her lashes,"If you did not discuss me, then what about his proposition?"

"He offered ten thousand for my assistance in returning this property to what he called 'the rightful owner', no questions asked."

She frowns and her brows contract in concern,"And did you have an answer for him?"

"I didn't have a chance. He withdrew the offer by drawing a gun and the negotiations turned rather hostile after."

She looks at him in shock; paling,"And yet, here you are to tell the tale," she clutches at her throat.

"He wasn't the only one with a gun. But, that didn't seem to matter much. Who or what exactly is he?"

"I- I'm sure I don't know what you mean. Or paths have crossed only once before. But, tell me, if his offer were genuine, what would your answer have been?" She keeps her hand on her delicate breastbone, but the inquiry of her eyes remains steady.

"Ten thousand dollars is a lot of money," he responds evenly, leaning forward.

"So, you would consider it."

"Ten thousand dollars is a lot of money," the tone of his response is as the first.

Her face all but crumbles and her hands fall nervelessly into her lap, two felled birds. She shrugs her shoulders slightly and in a small, defeated voice responds,"It is," she nods. "It is more than I could personally offer you, if that is how one must proposition for your loyalty."

"Ah," Brick breathes an acerbic sigh,"That's good coming from you. What have you ever given me beside money? Have you given me any of your confidence? Obviously not, since you have yet to offer the truth or any real facts that might be of any help."

She looks up, tear stained but truculent,"So, the war hero who fought for freedom and justice is now become a mercenary."

Brick snaps back at her,"Let's just say my preservation is not exactly negotiable at this point."

Their stares continue for a few moments, then Darya slides from the settee and on her knees beseeches him,"I've given you all the money I have, I now throw myself at your mercy, for without your help in this matter I am truly lost," she reaches out and grasps his hands that rest on his knees,"Please help me, Mr. Brick. How else can I possibly move you?"

The touch of her hands sends an unexpected shock up through his arms, shoulder, neck and into his head. Rapid images skim across his vision: that first sanguine smile, framed by her black veil, the heady scent of her perfume, the beguiling contours of her body, the exotic lilt of her timbre…. Their faces are close. He finds himself drifting, falling into her dark, opalescent eyes. Their breaths meet, their lips. His hands slip from under hers and cradle the back of her head, submerging into the ebony ocean of her hair. Their lips meet again and again and again.

He pulls back, still holding her head in his hands, his fingers sliding along under her jawline and with the back of his fingers he brushes the hair that has fallen onto her forehead. His eyes flicker across her upturned face. Then he starts and rises from the chair. He crosses to the desk and leans heavily on the edge. After a couple of deep breaths he mutters,"That was really professional." He turns back to her,"I've dealt with all kinds of liars, cheats and frauds and I'm willing to put everything aside that's happened so far, so consider yourself lucky. But, I've got to have more confidence in you than I do now."

"Please just give me a littler longer and then I'll be able to tell you everything I can."

"I've already stuck my neck out for you this far and I've no intention of going back on my offer, but you've got to convince me that you know what you're doing and not trusting to happenstance. Or counting on a fall guy. You don't have to trust me as long as you can persuade me to trust you."

He has crossed the room and is now looming over her. His fists are clenched as his his jaw. His eyes glitter fiercely down at her. She swallows hard and says in a subdued voice,"I should see Terranova first."

He stares at her as his mind checks a list: so far no mention of his seemingly unnatural appearance and abilities. As his secretary mentioned, no blood was found in the office, but some clumps of soil and sand and cigarette butts from the hallway ashtrays. Under the circumstances, Brick was willing to let the implications of that rest on the back burner for now. Other matters were obviously more pressing.

"Our last parting was not exactly amicable. Any idea how to get a hold of him?"

She squirms and looks down,"Yes, I know where to leave a message."

"Fine. We'll arrange a meeting on favorable ground for us tonight. Get dressed."

Forty-five minutes later, Darya is turned out in a green pin-striped ensemble with flared cuffs and knee-length skirt. Brick has her wait in the hallway for several minutes, then opens the outer-office door and ushers her in. He takes her hat and kid-skin gloves and seats her in the office reception area. "It's after regular business hours, so we can deal with him him as you like." Darya seems about to ask just what that might entail when there is a soft knock on the door. She stiffens and grips the chair and looks at Brick with apprehension. He squeezes her shoulder and smiles reassuringly at her,"Don't be frightened, nothing very bad is going to happen here."

He crosses to the door and opens it. Another dark, wide-brimmed hat, but a Navy blue Crombie coat this time hovers in the hallway. Terranova looks at Brick through the pair of dark glasses, then snorts irritably and enters. Brick closes the door behind him and watches as his two guests regard one another. The stunted figure doffs his hat, places it over his belly and gives a brief, stiff bow,"Delighted to see you again, Miss Markov."

Darya seems placated at this display of courtesy and relaxes back into the chair, but her eyes remain wary,"I'm sure you are, Augusto."

The dwarf's head was bald, fringed with wiry, gray hair that extended down to a short, but thick beard and mustache. In this unhurried light, the texture and pallor of his skin suggested nothing so much as baked clay. He turns his head slightly and addresses Brick,"There is a rather lengthy individual who has been prowling around these environs for the past few days who also seems to have an inordinate interest in the individuals who have inhabited this office. I came here in good faith, I had no real reason to expect -"

Darya grips the arm rests again and leans forward, alarmed,"He didn't follow you to my hotel, did he?" Her eyes seem all irises as she gapes at Brick. "No, I shook him before that. As Terranova says, he's been skulking around for days. He knows where to pick me up eventually." Darya leans back again but still exhibits discomfort as her eyes shift back and forth between the two others.

"So, only Miss Markov is actually acquainted with Mr. Pines," Brick reflects out loud. "Then how did the two of you…." he gestures from one to the other.

"We became acquainted in Honolulu. It seems we were both employed to acquire the object I mentioned before from our prospective…. 'owners'." He looks pointedly at Darya who glares back at him. "She was supposed to 'influence' a sailor but missed her inter-island connection and incurred the wrath of her employer. Enough to temporarily bring her into enough disfavor, that there was a price on her head. The fact that she remains above ground would seem to be a testament to her ability to reconcile with 'El jefe', yes?"

Darya casts her eyes down, her hands worry the arm rests,"There's…. been a reprieve. I just want to be shut of the whole affair. I am sorry I ever agreed -" She looks up at Terranova, intensely,"Are you sure you can get us ten thousand at a moments notice?"

"May I," Terranova gestures to another of the wooden chairs."Help yourself. I'll be over here," Brick replies. Terranova sits on a chair by the railing. Brick sits by his secretary's desk and rolls a cigarette.

"To answer your question: anytime during regular banking hours. But, why is that any of your concern? Do you have the item?"

Darya squirms in her chair, but eventually shakes her head,"No."

"Then my business is with Mr. Brick. In spite of our mutual misunderstanding on the first occasion of our acquaintance, my offer still stands."

"I mean to say I don't have it now, but soon, a day or two, maybe."

The squat figure grunted,"The sooner, the better. Considering what happened to Mr. Brick's partner, it would behoove us all -"

Brick starts up from his chair, scattering tobacco flakes,"What does Walter have to do with this?"

Terranova looks at him askance,"That is a question, as he was killed while garbed in your apparel."

Brick pauses and slowly works his way to the side of the desk closest to Terranova. "You are the one who tailed me to the parking lot, thinking I was Walter, so it seems to me you would be in the best position here to answer that question yourself."

Terranova scowls and looks from Brick to Darya and back,"Being a detective, Mr. Brick, I shouldn't have to remind you that Mr. Diamond met his demise because of his involvement with Miss Markov."

With this, Darya springs from her chair and rushes at Terranova,"How dare you! How dare you try to make me look like -'. She scrabbles at Terranova with her nails, he thrusts out his arm and clutches her throat with a mace-like fist. He rises from the chair and lifts her bodily, her legs flailing ineffectually in the air. Brick grasps the base of the lamp on Lorna's desk and flicks the switch on. He snaps the shade down on the desk and smashes the bulb. With his free hand he grips Terranova by the arm and Darya's feet scrape the floor as he plunges the now bare filament into the stout neck of the impish visitor.

There is loud slap of electrical discharge and the resulting burst hurls Terranova to the wall with a cry. Darya is flung back to her seat which tips and crashes to the floor. The lights flicker off. The only illumination is the thick dusk through the inner office windows. The air is suffused with thin smoke and the smell of burnt cork. Terranova clasps a hand over his neck and glares at Brick,"That's the second time you've laid hands on me!" His eyes flare and he seems about to rise from the floor, but he only manages to make it to his feet. He groans and rubs his neck.

"When your zapped, you'll take it and like it." Brick snarls as he slams the remains of the lamp on the desk. Trembling and breathing hard, he moves to Darya and helps to right her in the chair,"You OK, angel?" She rubs the back of her neck and nods shakily,"I – I think so..." He settles her in the seat, then turns and casts a pensive glance at Terranova. He crosses to the door to the inner office which he had left ajar. He reaches up and takes a heavy object down from over the door and crosses back to the wall and looks down at Terranova.

"I figure it was you lurking in the ashtrays in the hall outside the first time. Now before I start to make some mud pies, I suggest you come clean on what you know about Walt's death and -"

Just then, there is a loud pounding on the door. All three look up as Brick cradles a bucket of water in both hands over the recumbent Terranova. Brick growls,"Who the hell could -", he breaks off with an angry grunt and crosses to Darya. "If he moves, tip the whole thing in his face." He drags her within two feet of Terranova and places her hands on the bucket for quick application. "It's heavy," she groans. "I'll just be a second," he placates as he crosses to the hallway entrance.

Brick clocks the bulky shadows weaving across the frosted glass of the door highlighted by electric torch light and swears irritably under his breath. He takes a moment to compose himself then jerks the door open,"You guys pick a swell hours for a social call."

Maclane and Bond stand in the hallway. They rock restlessly on their heels. Bond says diffidently,"We'd like to talk with you, Lloyd."

"I don't have time now -"

"We're just adhering to your good advice, Brick," Maclane offers. Following every possible lead. Meticulous, that's us."

"I'm not accustomed to chewing my cabbage twice -" he starts to withdraw and close the door, but Bond reaches out and puts a hand on Brick's chest,"Now, don't be that way, Lloyd -"

Brick's eyes flash, his teeth click together and he grits out,"You're not trying to strong arm me, are you Tom?"

Bond pulls back with a sheepish chuckle,"Of course not, Lloyd, but we got a tip -"

"Oh, so that's it. An anonymous one, I'd bet. Was it a woman's voice?"

Bond flushes uncomfortably. Maclane gives a tight little smile,"There's talk that you and Walt's wife were stepping out on him and that's why he was put on the spot."

Brick's eyes glitter with annoyance,"Is that the hot tip that brought you up here?" Just then the building lights flicker on again. The officers turn of their bulky flashlights.

"Even money says that little blackout just now has something to do with you, too. Let us in."

Both Brick's and eyes and mouth turn down. He slowly shakes his head and starts to close the door when a scream and a loud crash emanate from the office behind him. The men in the hallway freeze, then Maclane presses a hand on the door," I guess we're going in." Brick steps aside,"I guess you are." The two officers plunge into the room. Brick closes the door and follows.

Darya Markov is huddled on the floor next to the chair she originally occupied. The bucket rolls about the floor, the office floor now awash with it's liquid contents. Terranova is nowhere to be seen. "What -", starts Maclane. "Where-" starts Brick when they are interrupted by another crash. This time the sound of breaking glass from the inner office.

The two policemen draw their guns and rush into Brick's office. Brick crosses to Darya and helps her to her feet. "Are you hurt?" She nervously shakes her head, 'No' and he helps her to sit down. Bond clomps back into the room, holstering his pistol. "The window's busted out, but there's no sign of anyone and we're five stories up."

Maclane enters also replacing his firearm."What could have caused someone to attempt such a death defying escape, I wonder?"

"Could he have gotten into one of the windows to another office?" Bond scratches his ponderous head.

"Doubtful. The only way someone could've disappeared from view that quickly would've been to kiss the pavement. What goes on here, Brick?"

"Miss Markov and I were in an interview with a Senor Gustavo Terranova. Miss Markov is a freelancer in my employ. Terranova claimed to have some information on Walt's murder. So, we asked him to meet us here." He calmly sits on the railing next to Darya. She looks at him quizzically, but remains mute and casts her eyes in wide-eyed innocence at the police.

The two officers slowly clock the room: the bucket, the water, the broken lamp and their gaze comes back to Lloyd who continues his unaffected mien. "Seems like you put the questions to him a little roughly," Mclane mutters. Brick smiles congenially,"Well, you know how that goes, Lieutenant."

"That still doesn't explain where he went."

"What happened here, Miss?", Bond tips his hat back and places his hands on his hips.

Darya looks startled, then looks to Brick for guidance. He drops down from the railing and interposes himself between her and the police,"I asked her to keep him company while I answered the door for you two. Considering his desperate flight, he must be holding something big. It's obvious he's not here. You're wasting time."

The two policemen glower at Brick, but he holds his ground. Then he feels something tug at his waist and he turns. Darya slowly rises from the chair and all but brushes him aside and confronts the two men:" Here", she says and tugs at the neck line of her garment. She cranes her head around slightly to reveal the blotches around her throat from Terranova's grip. The two detectives wince as they spy the bruises. Then their eyes lock in unison on hers. She seems to hold them breathlessly in her gaze as she continues to bare the defenseless hollow of her throat and breastbone.

"I - we could use your help", she rasps out softly. Then she demurely covers herself and retreats to Brick's side. The two gendarmes continue to stare at her. Then they slowly tip their hats and start to exit. "You haven't heard the last of this, Brick", the Lieutenant mutters as he closes the outer office door behind them.

"Hm. That was almost courtliness." He eyes her critically for a moment, then seats her,"Here". He crouches in front of her and takes her jaw lightly in one hand and turns her head and slowly assess the damage to her neck. "Any trouble breathing?", he asks while probing. She shakes her head slightly. "That's good. Still we might want to -" he breaks off as she reaches up and grasps his hand. She stares at him. He meets her gaze. He becomes immured in her dark eyes. Their heads drift together like two clouds, wafted on a zephyr of desire. Their mouths taste each other greedily.

Brick pulls back and holds her at arm's length. He cannot tear himself from her gaze at first. Then he swallows hard and tells her,"Wait here." Her eyes still fixed on him, he rises and crosses to his office. From his waistband he pulls a revolver he had secured when he first arrived. He flips on the light switch and moves towards the broken window. He stops and looks it over before crunching on the shards to peer outside. Satisfied, he steps back and cases the room. Then he heads for the outer office. But, before he gets to the door he turns and crosses quickly back into the room and aims and cocks the gun at his late partner's desk.

"Manos arriba!", he hisses. At first there is no response. Then what sounds like a sigh issues from under the desk. Slowly, and with much sounds of shuffling, the lumpen figure of Terranova rises. He complies, hands in the air, his eyes glittering, his mouth in a pout of amusement. "OK, I think it's past time we properly introduce ourselves: my name is Lloyd Brick, native of the planet Earth and you would be...?"

Terranova's smirk becomes a little wider, "Well, if you really must know. I would be... leaving."

Brick frowns in incomprehension, when suddenly a galaxy of stars explodes before his eyes and trails off into a sparkling shower of constellations in a Stygian sky.

"You know, you keep taking shots like that to the head, we're gonna end up partners again sooner rather than later."

Brick feels his heartbeat throbbing inside his head. He opens his eyes: darkness. Then a light flares and he smells sulfur. He turns his head and spies a figure in a trench coat and hat with his back to him, drawing on a cigarette. "Has it occurred to you yet, that maybe you're dealing with forces you don't understand?" Brick tries to respond. He is lying on his back and can just raise his head when the figure suddenly crouches and looms over him,"These people are not jake. Don't forget Chinatown." And with that the figure stands and strolls slowly away. He might even be chuckling.

6

---◆---

Disoriented

B rick's eyes flutter open. When they focus he realizes he is staring at his bedroom ceiling. Still not convinced of his being conscious, he slowly turns his head to take in the room. This causes an ice pack which had been propped on his head to slide off. He reflexively grabs it, then leans up on one elbow. With a groan he reapplies the ice pack to the back of his neck and continues to scan the room, no longer suspicious of his cognizance.

The lamp by his bedside is the only one in the room burning and he smells her rather than sees her at first: Darya comes slinking out of the shadows. She is wearing a light terry cloth robe of his. She carries a glass of water in one hand and is cupping something in the other fist. She sits at the edge of the bed and exchanges the ice pack for the glass of water, then places two aspirin tablets in the other hand.

Their gaze locks and they remain wordless while he takes the offered aspirin and water. She hands him the ice pack and eases him back on the bed:"How are you feeling?" "Like Oswald in *Ghosts*. Or am I through the looking glass?" he replies as he looks her steadily in the eye. "Here", she says and takes his hand which she holds while gently massaging the web between thumb and forefinger. "I know that's supposed to help the headache, but what would really help would be some answers -" he starts to rise, she gently eases him back.

She takes both his hands in hers and fixes him with her gaze. She continues to gently massage his hands while she murmurs softly:"Not now. Rest. You've been through much these last few days. Give yourself a chance to heal, to rest, rest..." He lies back,"What time is it? How long have I been -" "Shh... not long." She plants a forefinger on his lips." It's getting late, there's nothing out there that can't keep for tonight... rest... let me ..." her hand moves to his forehead and she continues to caress him. In spite of his agitation, Brick begins to feel drowsy, indeed.

His lids at half mast, he nevertheless cannot avert his gaze from hers. He feels the vertiginous maelstrom of her dark eyes begin to eclipse everything else in his field of vision. Then her breath floats over him and he can feel the swell of her breasts as she drapes herself on him. Their mouths verge and respond hungrily. One hand strokes the small of her back, the other is engulfed in the dark cascade of her hair. They writhe together for a few moments, then she presses her hands to his chest and while never taking her eyes off of him, sits up, sliding her hands over her body peeling back the robe. Brick's eyes move to the chiaroscuro of the bow and flexure of her lissome frame revealed in the single, soft light. She tosses her opulent locks, smiles at him and reaches over and turns out the lamp. The last thing Brick remembers thinking is: "Hey, I think my headache's gone."

The night fog has lifted and there are gray glimmers of dawn under the morning marine layer. Brick wakes to the smell of brewed coffee. He sits up slowly, flexing his neck, sits at the side of the bed, stretches and scratches. He slowly pads towards the scent of caffeine and stops short when he sees the pot on the stove, one cup and saucer on the counter and a note propped up on same. Brick pours the coffee, sugar, then sits at the table and opens the note: 'Darling. I know that as much as I am in dire need of your strong protection, you must remain free to follow wherever your leads take you. I will move to another location and let you know where I land as soon as I am settled. Yours, Darya.'

Brick sighs and crumples the note. He finished his coffee, tosses the note in the trash and checks the time. He will have to hustle to make it to his appointment in the east bay. He dresses quickly and when finished, calls the driver he had used to take him to Hunter's Point, meeting him behind the Podesta Baldocci florist on Grant Avenue to shake any potential tails. Satisfied that his maneuver was successful keeping his venture unobserved, he tries to cobble together pieces of narrative from the previous evening's exploits, but his headache returns and instead he rolls down the window and lets the morning coastal air gently buffet him.

'Amphibious is right,' he thinks as he spies the hundreds of landing craft arrayed in front of the hardly completed grandstand of the race track. From the highway, sitting here by the bay, they resemble nothing so much as large, prehistoric creatures heeding the call to gather and spawn by the seaside. Ten minutes later he is near the intersection of Buchanan and Gilman streets, crushing out a cigarette as he is approached by a powder blue Navy shore patrol jeep. A stocky, solidly built, sandy-haired young man emerges and immediately his resemblance to Brick's new associate is apparent.

"Mr. Brick," the young Lieutenant says as he extends his hand in greeting. "Lieutenant." They shake. "I've got to make this quick."

"I didn't think you were an MP."

"Definitely not, I've got to get this back to the motor pool before I get someone in dutch."

"OK. Spill it."

"I found it on the carrier *Independence*. It was after we had towed it to Pearl and were inspecting the damage from testing. Never reported it to command so..." he shrugs. "Found it sticking out of sand on deck near one of the funnels," he shakes his head in amazement. "I cabled my old Professor at Cal - I was hoping I could get a scholarly opinion on it before mentioning it to command, because it was so odd to find it there. I'm sure you know how proprietary the military can be."

Brick gives a tight smile and nods in acquiescence and encouragement. "So, I took the jar out to Berkeley and left it with the professor. And that night, as he was closing the lab, he came across someone who had broken in and was attacked. The next thing he knew, the jar was gone – the only thing missing."

"Is there any reason to believe your cable was intercepted or monitored or that you were followed to the university? Where did you conceal it all this time?"

The young sailor scratches his head,"No. It never occurred to me that anyone one else would even be interested. I kept it in my footlocker, then carried it on shore in my duffle. It was only in my possession less than a week and not more than a few hours once we docked at Hunter's Point. I never said word one to anyone, except the Professor."

"Did the Professor describe the assailant?" The glare off of the water is beginning to exacerbate his headache as the marine layer thins. He rubs his temple as he listens.

"It was dark, but he said whoever it was, he was large, strong and – I thought this was interesting – had a peculiar odor, that the Professor couldn't quite place, but it was very... distinctive."

Brick nods noncommittally. Eugene checks his watch and grimaces,"I'm sorry, Mr. Brick, but I really need to -" The young man fumbles in his breast pocket for a moment, then produces a folded piece of paper:"Here's the dimensions and a rough description of it." He hands the note to Brick, who unfolds it.

"The jars are made of either stone or pottery and this one was no exception, but for the fact that it seems to be reinforced with something harder. Now, it may be from a later period, where they kept the viscera in the bodies and just made dummy jars that were never hollowed out, but if you shake it; there definitely seems to be something inside." Brick nods and folds up the paper and stashes it inside his suit pocket.

The young man looks down and licks his lips,"Thank you for... I never thought this would become so – involved. Please, the last thing I want is to get my cousin in trouble or anyone -"

Brick waves him off,"I don't know that you did the right thing, but I've got a hell of an associate and I don't intend to let her down. Carry on, Lieutenant. We'll catch up later." Eugene moves to his jeep, enters and speeds away. Brick motions to his driver who has parked several yards away.

The driver calls out,"Where to?" "The office, pronto." and before Brick can even get the door closed, they are headed in the opposite direction, back to the city.

Thirty minutes later, Brick barges into his office and finding Lorna behind her desk - as he expected – starts issuing instructions:" Get on the blower and check with your double x network to see if we can find where Miss Markov has landed, I'll check back in an hour. Sorry about the mess -"

"Lloyd, what in heaven's name happened -"

"Just get maintenance up here ASAP. I'm sure they know the way -"

"Already done. Did you see Eugene?"

"Already done, partner. Things are starting to coalesce, I 'll know better when I get back."

"From where this time?"

"To see how the fortune cookie crumbles," he says as he swings out the door.

Half an hour later, Brick stands on the corner across from a storefront bearing a sign that reads: China Importing Company - Wholesale Chinese Porcelain. He pops two yellow pills into his mouth which he acquired at his previous stop and dry swallows them. The headache has become an insistent backseat driver. Around him, the daily routine of Chinatown swirls and eddies around him: young schoolgirls in plaid skirts, saddle shoes and bobby socks, wiry waiters carrying trays of bao on their heads, a young blond in a fur coat negotiating the press as quickly as she can on her high heels. He cinches up his belt, takes a big breath and crosses the street.

After entering, he slips past the slightly dusty and crowded shelves to the rear of the store. Before the ancient clerk at the register can protest he skirts the sales counter and pulls back the curtain to the inner office. He immediately collides with an Asian figure, who, although half a head shorter must outweigh Brick by eighty pounds. A buzzcut and a pencil thin mustache accentuating the down turn of his mouth brought a menacing air to the flat reptilian stare.

Brick clears his throat and says,"Fong sent me."

After a moment, the stolid figure turns and crosses to a door at the back of the room. Placing his hand on the knob he nods for Brick to follow and opens the door. Brick does as instructed and the silent sentinel allows him entry then closes the door behind them. Before them is a vast room arrayed with innumerable racks all populated with various sizes and configurations of porcelain. The attendant moves past Brick and the detective follows. His gaze is arrested by the sunlight filtering through the skylights, bathing the china in a warm radiance that would not be out of place in an egg hatchery.

In the middle of the room is a circular area curtained off from the rest. Brick is lead to an opening which the attendant parts, then bows slightly and gestures for Brick to enter. Brick steps in and the drape is dropped behind him. Brick looks up to see – what might be a grizzly bear in silk robes. Almost seven feet tall including the red fez perched on his massive, loaf-like head, with long nails on hands like frying pans, it would not be unreasonable to conclude that one was ushered into an ursine den.

"Either you're the man I've come to see or you're laughing boy's big brother," he says as he nods back towards the curtains. The giant permits a small smile,"Man Fat, at your service." He gives the fist/palm salute, Brick nods in acknowledgment. His large host then gestures towards a freestanding coat rack. Brick nods, "Thanks" and crosses to the rack and places his hat on top. As he starts to remove his coat, the behemoth helps him shrug out of it and hangs it up for him, then gestures to a silk upholstered oak chair. Brick marvels at the dexterity with which he manipulates objects in spite of the prodigious nails on each hand. He crosses and seats himself.

"I am given to understand that you are a man of some integrity and that I may be of some help to you regarding your partner's sudden demise." In the soft, ambient light, Brick can tell in spite of the manicured eyebrows and Fu Manchu mustache, his host was certainly not Asian. Brick understood that people are rarely what they seem, but this crazy caper seems to be taking it to extremes.

Man Fat pours two drinks of bourbon into tumblers from a Lume cut glass decanter. The receptacle looks almost like a thumbtack in his large mitts.

"Maybe, but we should start with a motive, I can probably figure it out from there," Brick offers.

"And what would that be?"

"A certain Egyptian artifact that went missing from across the bay a couple of nights ago."

The gargantuan pseudo-Chinese pauses in his ministrations only slightly. He crosses to Lloyd, hands him his drink, and raises his glass in a toast," Here's to plain speaking and clear understanding."

"Cheers." They drink. Then Man Fat begins a slow circuit to his chair. "We begin well, sir. Straight to the point, no beating about the bush." He stops and places a hand on the back of his chair."How familiar are you with ancient Egyptian burial rites and practices?"

"Straight to the point: I know that after their embalming techniques improved they stopped placing internal organs in jars."

Fat nods in appreciation,"An untold number created and now scattered about the globe in museums in private collections... but only one – unknown, save for a very few who covet such rarities - is believed to be merely a vessel for …. a passage to immortality." He chuckles seemingly at the notion and moves in front of the chair. "And how well versed are you in Egyptian mythology?"

"I believe I'm familiar with most of the major deities."

"Then, please allow me to add what may or may not be a bit of apocrypha for your conjecture. In ancient Egypt, the cult of the god Osiris, who was chiefly a god of regeneration and rebirth, had a particularly strong interest in the concept of immortality. As ruler of the dead, Osiris was also called "king of the living", since the ancient Egyptians considered the blessed dead, 'the living ones'.

The colossus settles himself in sections in the large, sleek, purple wing-backed chair opposite. The seat creaks audibly under his massive girth as he continues," Osiris was considered not only a judge in the afterlife, but also the underworld agency that granted all life."

He sets his own drink down next to him on the cherry and maple wood table and from inside his voluminous *hanfu* he removes a small flask, uncaps it and pours a measure of fluid of a viscous nature into his tumbler. Returning the flask to his robe, he absently picks up a crystal swizzle stick and gently stirs the drink with a minute flexing of his fingers.

He sips his humorous cocktail,"He was also described as 'He Who is Permanently Youthful'. The kings of Egypt were associated with Osiris in death: as Osiris rose from the dead, so would they."

His voice drops into a hoarse whisper as he intones,"In the year three thousand B.C. the capitol of Old Egypt was at the mouth of the Nile delta and called among other things, Djed-sut meaning, 'everlasting places', it eventually acquired the more familiar appellation of Memphis."

He rolls the edge of the glass between his huge hands,"It is said that Ptah; demiurge of Memphis, god of craftsmen and architects made a golden device for the assimilation and resurrection rituals. This device was supposedly shaped like a free-tailed bat, which would, when applied to the body of the supplicant, allow them to inherit eternal life through a process of imitative magic. But the experiment proved that eternal was easier to achieve than life."

He leans in and in an ominous voice intones," The first test subjects they tried it on became neither alive nor dead, but continued on. Compelled to prolong their wretched existence by consuming the blood of living creatures. It is largely assumed that these unfortunates were either exterminated or succumbed to the many weaknesses and violent changes that were wrought in their physiology."

Eyes twinkling with delectation he leans back and continues in a more casual manner,"And it just so happened that the center of another important cult was also in Memphis, that of Im Ho Tep, who was Chancellor to the King of Upper Egypt and his successor. Also he attained the elevated status of High Priest and of Chief Architect and Physician and one of very few commoners to be accorded divine status after death. And who, for reasons unknown, apparently was not consulted or informed of this contrivance."

"Ah, I smell a turf war brewing."

The fat man beamed and nodded, bouncing his jowls,"Indeed, Im Ho Tep is said to have been beyond insulted and being regarded as 'the son of Ptah', now covets this prize and in a disingenuous but, logical offer as he is also Maker of Vases in Chief, promises to make a glorious 'container' for this singular device."

"How could things help but go south, when you throw in a family feud?"

"Ha! Your choice of phrase is well-turned. You see Osiris was not fooled for a moment by Im Ho Tep's invitation and instructed Ptah to agree, but then also instructed him to make a container for it that might escape easy detection -"

"And what could be more appropriate or ubiquitous than a canopic jar..."

"Indeed. A stroke of genius. The only distinguishing feature was to be a small insignia or glyph etched in the surface that supposedly could only be seen in special circumstances. In any case, it must have sent to the upper Nile, because the next mention of anything like it surfaces around the year seven-eighty when al-Mahdi restored part of the Suez canal. And yes, canals have long been a feature there, though the only significant one wasn't constructed until Darius the Great.""

"So it was archived, as it were."

"Perhaps. In any case, it would seem that as time passed, no one who may have had possession of it knew if it's purported significance, since there is no record of it ever having been returned to Memphis or to anyone's possession. In fact the next mention of it is in the tenth century: a missive from al-Adil to his brother Saladin, when they were fortifying the eastern frontier of Egypt against the Crusaders. Al-Adil was given the task of ending the blockade of Raynald of Chatillon in the Red Sea. But, again it is only a reference with no indication of it's significance nor disposition."

"Curious. But, obviously not the end of it's odyssey."

"No, sir. And your reference to Odysseus is quite apt, because there seem to be oblique references to the item both at Thebes and Abu Simbel. Which makes perfect sense since both locations temples were dedicated to the god, Ptah."

Brick pinches his lower lip,"In any case, the dingus seems to be moving further south..."

"And east," Man Fat says.

He sighs, takes a drink, then looks to a distant corner of the room and his voice takes on an inflection of bemusement:"Trying to bridge the gap in the span of eons is an absurdity, but I will tell you that in two centuries that part of the world would be plundered and occupied by the Bedouin and it would be another two centuries after that before another credible mention of the artifact would surface."

When his eyes track back to Brick, his face falls:"You're amused, sir? You think perhaps my tale is nothing more substantial than a lotus eater's fantasy?"

Brick stirs and smiles wryly:"Let's get a little closer to the present day and we'll see how far I tumble."

The occidental/oriental, smiled in return and raised his glass in salute,"Your honest skepticism is not only warranted, but to be commended," He drinks, sets his glass down on the table and wriggles his bulk in the audibly complaining chair and continues:" Now, the last Mamluk sultan decided to fortify against the Portuguese in the Red Sea, which caused the area to fall to the Ottoman empire a century later. Two more centuries later, however, the area sees an upturn in it's fortunes. By then a twenty vessel fleet would sail annually from Suez to Jeddeh, the port of the holy city of Mecca and... the trading gateway from Egypt... to India." With this he settles back with an expectant lift to his conspicuously sculpted eyebrows.

Brick nods,"So, this may be how it moved further east."

"That much we can surmise, but as to how, when and by whom...," he spreads his humongous hands in a gesture of abdication.

"You've still got a couple of centuries and several thousand miles to go."

Man Fat plops his hands on his knees and bows his head. He lifts his gaze and with an apologetic smile explains,"A century later there were rumors to the effect that it had fallen into the hands of Napoleon, but there are many difficult giving any credence to that considering what we know today. It was just over a decade ago that the search for this instrument was made aware to a few souls who had harbored it's scant but scintillating history for generations."

He dips the prodigious nail of his left little finger into his drink and licks the drops absently,"A preoccupation with the occult of the ancients by one Heinrich Himmler, set out waves of innervation to networks and connections long thought to have been as dormant as the pharaohs."

"I remember a conversation with an O.S.S. operative about how the Nazi's obsession with the cult even brought them to covet ancient Jewish artifacts." Brick tugged at an earlobe."And the possibility of an immortal army of the 'un-dead' would square nicely with their concept of *das Herrenvolk.*

Brick's huge host tilts his head and nods,"You're a man to my liking, a man of many resources and nice judgment. You begin to believe me a little?"

Brick shrugs and sips his drink,"Except for your story beginning with gods and demi-gods, there may be some veracity to the yarn."

The fat man's lips curl in an impish grin,"The origin story *is* problematic in the ascendancy of mono-theism, but there is more than enough evidence to suggest that the artifact does indeed exist." He flips his hand in dismissal and leans forward animatedly,"Supernatural properties or no, the mere fact that this is a treasure – a singular one - in gold, from ancient Egypt, makes the thing practically invaluable."

"I like your choice of adjective. If it's value is nearly inestimable, then the higher the price can be asked for it's possession."

Man Fat snaps his head back and roars with laughter; the entire room seems to quake with his mirth,"By Gad, sir, you're a chap worth knowing, an amazing character." He settles back, sets the drink down on the side table to gauge Brick's response. Behind the poker face he has so carefully constructed which usually kept him a formidable enigma to others, Brick's frontal lobes felt as if they would melt; the implications of what this could mean, if at all true. But, how could it be? He takes a long pull on his excellent whiskey.

"Yes. You see it. I thought you would." Fat is leaning forward in his chair, eyes wide with urgency and desire. He seems to sense that his excitement is too revealing for after a moment he relapses to his former languid self and settles back against the chair, hands folded like a steeple under his chins.

"Let's suppose this *is* what all the fuss is about. How does my late partner come into it? This wouldn't have anything to do with extracurricular activities during the war, would it?" Brick asks pointedly.

From the twitch in the arched eyebrows of his host, Brick seems to have struck a nerve. He presses a little further and leans in,"I imagine he had a nice little arrangement here in Chinatown. His position and reputation on the force has always been an asset at first, but now -"

"Eventually it becomes it's opposite as circumstances change, does it not, Mr. Brick? And then measures must be taken; an inevtibale conclusion." Something in his smirk seems to suggest to Brick a certain implied complicity. He starts to feel a little queasy. Perhaps he should cut the drinking after those pills.

"And this – treasure, is the transgression that earned him a slow boat to Duat."

The fleshy fingers spread to the air in a gesture of incomprehension,"He was knowledgeable regarding the item, but was certainly also well aware that said item was being acquired by – other channels. He was to have no part in it."

Brick sits back contemplatively,"So, you think he was trying to horn in on this deal? He did seem rather more animated that afternoon than I had seen in quite some time." He draws an index finger back and forth across his upper lip."And he got what you think he deserved. I wonder how the D.A. will feel about such an arrangement."

The prodigious face crumples in pain,"My dear sir. Have I ever yet implied that I was in any way responsible for his fate? If that were so, would I be talking to you about any of this? No, I am telling you all this because his death is our common cause. As you must know, the item is still unaccounted for."

"So, if you don't have it – then who does?"

One lacquered nail lashes heavenward,"That is the question. And who could be more suited to find out than a skilled professional such as yourself?"

"Is that an offer?" He vision begins to swim a little, but his headache seems to be receding to a dim echo.

"I am in a position with immense resources, which can be made welcome to any of my colleagues as the need arises."

"I'm already up to my ears in clients and apparent competitors."

"Marvelous to have so many options. America is indeed the land of opportunity. So, now the question becomes, which one of them will you represent?"

"Not necessarily."

Again the eyebrows gambol,"Yet another choice?"

Brick leans back casually in the chair, crosses his legs and cocks a thumb at his chest,"There's me."

There is a pause as the eyebrows seem to hover a little higher. Then the corners of Fat's mouth turn up as he exhales," I do like a man who tells you right out that he's looking out for himself. Don't we all?" he shrugs. "Who could trust a man who says he's not?"

"So, find the jar, find the killer."

"Apparently. But, be warned Mr. Brick. There are forces involved in this that are likely beyond your scope. Let your partner's avarice be a lesson in ill-advised ambition."

Brick rises and crosses to the coat rack and retrieves his garments."I'll keep that in mind." As he approaches the curtain, the thickset amanuenses appears and parts it for him. Brick eyes him as he shrugs into his coat,"He family?"

"Toshi? No, he just does the odd job for me now and then."

Brick replaces the hat on his head, takes a deep breath and addresses the barrel-chested Japanese: "Lead on, yojimbo."

This time, his host forms the fist/palm salute in parting. Brick tips the brim of his hat in acknowledgment and follows the large subordinate out. Without the solid back of his guide to follow, the monochromatic redundancy of the room's interior seems an impenetrable maze.

Once outside the brisk autumn peninsula air whips some of the cobwebs from his brain as he takes a trolley back towards his office. He walks a few blocks in a further attempt to alleviate the effects of the alcohol with the pills he was given. "Should've known better," he thinks."Most likely an opium derivative," he muses as he enters his office building.

When he gets to the office, Lorna is standing by the door with a piece of note paper in her hand which she extends to him,"She's at the Alexandria Hotel. Suite 12C. Oh, and the reason you two were so conveniently 'rescued' by the police last night, is because they we're tipped off." Brick looks up from the note, sharply,"So, they claimed. I've no doubt it was -"

"The grieving widow. Apparently she had the office staked out and saw you and Miss Markov and Mr. Terranova go in. She dropped a dime on what she said were the 'conspirators who killed her husband'."

"Well, I'll be...'" he stops and stares at her,"How did you find out about-" Lorna taps the side of her nose and replies,"There are networks that women have that men shall never understand or access."

"Hm. Apparently."

She hands him another note,"The D.A.'s office called wants to see you this afternoon at four. I would suggest you stop by Clarence's office beforehand to brush up on your civics."

"Aye-aye. And your dance card is full too, partner?"

"Don't you worry about my end," she says as she crosses to her desk and retrieves her purse from the back of her chair. "We should stop meeting like this. People are going to think we're estranged," she crosses to the door and opens it. Just as she ducks out,"Maintenance has come and gone. They want to be put on a retainer after yesterday. Don't forget to lock up." And with that she is gone.

7

The Fall Guy

He arrives at the door to 12C and knocks three times, rests, then knocks twice, then once; an arranged signal. After a few moments the door is opened. She stands before him in a pink tea-dress with white ribbon print pattern towards the hem and on the sleeves, accentuated with sequins. "I'm sorry I didn't -" Brick takes her by the shoulder and steers her into the room.

He guides her to the divan and pushes her into the seat. She sits, with an anguished expression, silently fretting as Brick removes his hat and coat and takes two cigarettes from the mirrored box on the coffee table. He puts both in his mouth, lights them with the formidable chrome table lighter and seats himself next to her and offers her one. She takes it and brushes her hair back with trembling fingers.

"I believe I've got the what and why. What I really need to know now is: who?" Her body tenses next to his. Then she rises from the sofa and crosses to the mantelpiece and slightly rearranges the flowers in the crystal vase set there. Then she moves to a window and flicks the curtain back to glance at the weather, then moves back to Brick, rearranges a cushion on the sofa, then taps her ash into the tray on the table and remains standing, staring at nothing in particular.

"You picked a nice set of playmates."

Her eyes turn to him. After a pause she stubs out the cigarette and exhales,"Only that sort is interested in – that sort of thing."

"How bad a spot are you in?"

"As bad as could be," comes the reply as she folds her arms and hugs herself. "I'm not heroic. I know that there are worse things than death."

"Who killed Walt? Pines? Terranova?"

"I don't know," she says as she rocks slightly back and forth on her feet.

"A few nights ago when this whole dizzy affair started I was accosted by some local hoods, who managed to get the drop on me, thinking I was my partner." He leans forwards and taps his ash into the table tray. "But, before they could do some serious damage, someone else showed up. I've sneaking suspicion it was Terranova who intervened. Why would he do that, unless there was something he thought he needed from me?"

She is actually starting to pace now."I -I don't know. Are you sure? It could've been someone else."

"Someone else...", Brick echoes as he considers the other figure who appeared then. He shakes his head,"No. His aura is pretty distinctive. What happened in Hawaii? How did the news of the bat get out?"

She stops moving and turns her astonished and frightened face to him. She stares, purses her lips, lowers her head and shakes it negatively,"I don't know how things like this come to the attention of others. I was just hired to..." Her eyes shift away.

"You're not going to run around the room, straightening things up again, are you?"

She starts, but then gives a small laugh and runs her hand through her hair," No. No." She sits again on the divan. "I was hired to retrieve the item from a sailor in Pearl Harbor. That is all I was told."

"By whom?"

"I don't know. It's a blind drop. I get a signal to pick up the information and my payoffs in a different place every time. It was set up by my uncle years ago, I have not seen him in years."

Brick takes out the paper with the description of the canopic jar and hands it to her,"Is this a fair approximation of your target?" She takes it and scans it briefly,"Yes. But, I've still never actually seen it."

"The sailor; blond, blue-eyed, about five-nine -"

"Yes, a young Lieutenant."

"And Terranova. He said you two crossed paths in Hawaii."

She squirms slightly and in doing so closes the gap between them on the divan. "He was the reason I missed my connection to Pearl Harbor. He appeared out of nowhere near the women's restroom and held me there until my flight had departed."

"Then you both tailed him to the mainland. So, he was to stop you, not go after the jar himself?"

"I don't know. I just knew that my best chance at that point was to get to San Francisco and try to intercept the Lieutenant here. I figured if he were to leave the confines of the military, it would be easier to…. approach him."

"You have no idea who engaged you. What about Terranova?"

She shakes her head then lowers it on his shoulder and lets out a long sigh. "And then this Pines person shows up and -"

"And it was just a coincidence that you just happened to choose an agency where someone was connected with your deal was situated."

She stiffens, raises her head and looks at him,"Pines isn't just a threat, he's a mystery to me as well. It would not be in my best interests to be remain ignorant of his intentions while I am still obligated to fulfill my end of the contract." She reaches up and brushes his hair back from his forehead,"Why would I go anywhere else and risk even more people knowing of the real object of everyone's desire?" She smiles and her eyes dilate. Brick inhales her perfume and begins to relax involuntarily and leans back, "Either he or Terranova are associated with the Triads, though. That much I can be sure of. I just wish I had time to figure out the 'what' of Senor Terranova instead of the 'who'."

He rubs his face with his hands in exasperation and fatigue. She takes his hands away and holds them as she looks deeply into his eyes," You are an unusual man, a man of curiosity, and integrity or you could not do what you do and have succeeded at it. You'll find a way."

His head lolls back on the sofa, "If I could only rest this damned head a minute or two, I might be able to make some sense out of this…. Pandora's box…." He closes his eyes wearily. She releases his hands and strokes his brow,"Poor head." After a few moments she leans over and places her mouth over his. They kiss long and deeply. After a minute he he takes her by the shoulders and holds her at arm's length. His eyes work over her critically. He feels his heart thrum and lurch in his breast. Then with a grunt he rises from the sofa and crosses the room to retrieve his hat and coat.

"As much as I'd love to convalesce with you, I've got to keep moving. Too many plates in the air." She follows him to the door and leans languorously on the wall next to the door. He turns and takes her face in his hand,"You know where to come for help if you think you need it. And when it suits you." He drops his hand and turns and exits. She starts from the wall, her mouth open to reply, but snaps it shut with pique after the door slams shut.

Brick exits the elevator and as he does he spies a lanky figure sitting on a divan from which the elevators can be observed. At the moment he seems engrossed in the news paper he is apparently reading. Brick strolls over casually and seats himself on the nearest armchair to the divan.

Now at this close range Brick could take in the details: tall, angular and hirsute, he did indeed seem to sport a 'round the dial five o'clock shadow as Darya had suggested. The clothes were good, well pressed, but not new. His elongated snout is deeply burrowed in the paper as Brick casually intones,"Oh, good. I thought I'd lost you." The paper crackles slightly and with a measured pace suggesting a powerful restraint, lowers. The prominent nose emerges and just above them, deep brown eyes that seem to stay focused somewhere in the space between the two men.

"Are you addressing me?"

"I think, considering our past relationship that we get acquainted, Jeff. Or is it, Mutt?"

"What? Are you kiddin' me, Jack?"

"I'll let you know when I am. You're a long way from Glassboro, kid. Get the bum's rush?"

"Keep asking for it and your gonna get it. But good. Shove off."

And with that he gives the paper a little rattle and returns his gaze to the pages. Brick leans in and responds evenly,"You're not in the pine barrens now, punk. You're in my burg."

"Fuck off."

"People loose teeth talkin' like that. You wanna hang around, you'd better exhibit some manners."

The paper only snaps between the two lean hands and is accompanied by an annoyed grunt in response. Brick rises to escalate the encounter, but spies a pot-bellied, gray-haired man in a dark brown suit standing by the cigar-stand. He waves to the man who catches the movement and hails back. He crosses the room and Brick steps out to meet him.

"Hello, Jasper."

"Hello, Lloyd. Tough break about, Walt." He offers a Lloyd a cigarette which he takes and lights it for him. Lloyd nods his thanks, and then nods towards the divan,"We'll just have to muddle through without, I guess. Say, what do you let cheap gunmen hang around your lobby for, scaring off clients with their heaters bulging in their clothes?"

Jasper's genial, puffy face suddenly slackens as he turns his now hardened gaze towards the divan. Both older men step in as Jasper says flatly,"Either state your business here or get out." The paper slowly lowers and is set aside as the long-limbed character rises and merely glares at both men.

"Well, I guess that means you're takin' the air. Beat it. And don't come back," the house dick says, flatly. Lloyd exhales a plume of smoke into the taller man's face.

The dark stranger glares at the two of them briefly and sniffs,"I won't forget you guys." Then slowly turns and stalks out.

"What was that about?" Jasper asks. Brick shrugs,"I dunno. Just spotted him. Do me a favor and call my office and tell my partner to relocate 12C, pronto!", he yells over his should as walks quickly to the same exit Pines used.

Jasper waves in acknowledgment and reaches for the phone,"Sure thing!" He picks up the phone to get an outside line then stops and exclaims,"Partner?" He shrugs and then continues with the call.

Brick reaches the lobby entrance and catches site of Pines as he strides away, hands deep in pockets. Brick weaves through the early afternoon foot traffic always keeping his subject just in view. Pines just seems to be fuming at first, just plowing briskly ahead, but after two blocks he slows and actually starts to cast glances over his shoulder. Brick manages to avoid his gaze, but starts to drop further behind in order to do so.

It is with some relief that Brick sees him approach the taxicab stand in front of the Sir Francis Drake hotel and lever himself into one. Brick skips quickly across the street and follows suit,"Follow that cab!", he enjoins as he clambers into the back of the idling vehicle. The driver responds with

with an alacrity that seems to enliven her whole demeanor,"You got it, handsome!" And she lurches into traffic, spilling Brick against the back seat.

Some thirty minutes later, Brick is watching the elongated figure of Pines dismiss his cab and lope along Old Alameda Point towards a large ship berthed inside the breakwater. It is a singular sight: what appears to be a 'Liberty Ship' is tethered there, but where the loading boom and hold hatches would normally be situated on the aft decks, there is a massive trellis-like structure which seems to be encased in glass: a giant atrium. He would like to question someone local about this vision, but decides against arousing any suspicion at this juncture. Besides he had only just enough time to get back to the city and confer with his attorney before his date with the District Attorney. He orders the cab to return to the city post haste.

He has the taxicab stop at the corner of Market and Seventh. "I'll be back in ten. The pert brunette flicks her finger at the meter,"I'll be countin' the minutes," then tips her hat down over her eyes, crosses her arms over her bosom and slides down in the seat behind the wheel. Inside, Brick strides up the stairs rather than wait on the elevator. Once at the top floor he ambles down the hall to the last door on the right, catches his breath, swears he'll cut out the tobacco one of these days. He leans on the doorknob, twists it and enters.

In the mote filled sunlight cast from the windows, a not-so-young and rather plump red head is twirling a lock of hair with the fingers of one hand while the other holds up a dime store novel in front of her heavily powdered face. She doesn't look up.

"Is he in?"

Snapping her chewing gum, she merely nods once and the hand in her hair releases long enough to jerk it's thumb in the direction of the inner office door, before returning to it's tonsorial teasing. Brick responds,"Thanks", and with a small smirk crosses to the door and enters without knocking.

As he closes the door behind him, a sallow faced man in suspenders and sleeve garters looks up from behind his desk,"It's about time", he growls around the corona cigar wagging in his lips. Brick looks at him, but keeps his hand on the doorknob to indicate his intention of a brief interlude.

"If you're referring to my partner's demise, then yes, I suppose, but that's what I've come about, because the D.A. and I are having tea today and I need to know if I can use the sanctity of client privilege to keep them at bay if it should come to that."

The attorney places both elbows on the top of the paper cluttered desk and cracks his knuckles,"Why not? It's not a court trial. You've gotten away with more than that before."

"I know, but things are rather thick this time, I think they wanted Walt and I -"

"Walt's widow stopped by."

Brick's hand leaves the doorknob,"What? When?" He steps further into the room,"Why?"

"Yesterday. And I could end up in San Quentin for telling you this -"

"You'd have plenty of clients as company, so?"

"She claims that Walt called her and told her he might not be coming home because he had a date with a girl at the St. Mark's – you know, him and his so-called sense of humor..."

"Sure. And?"

"So, she stakes out the St. Mark and sees him on the job tailing a couple – one of them the girl she said she saw you with the other night."

Brick's jaw drops in incredulity,"Jesus, these women!" The another thought occurs to him:"Then if she was following him, she must have seen -"

The attorney holds his hand up in abeyance,"She said after the couple parted she watched her husband continue after the man and they both made their way around the corner. Satisfied her husband was just ragging her about the date, as usual, she then went to your place, but you weren't at home. So, she drove around for a while, then went to the flickers on Powell Street; the one that stays open past midnight, then decided against seeing you, had a bite to eat at Tait's and went home for the night."

"And you believe her?"

The attorney spreads his hands in uncertainty. Brick steps in closer.,"Well, by then she must have noticed her husband wasn't home."

The attorney nods,"She took the car out again and said it was then that she decided to go by your place after all."

"Must've been down to Stockton Street checking out Walt's corpse by then." He rubs his chin thoughtfully,"What a comedy of errors. She go home again after she found out that I wasn't?"

"Yep. And while she was undressing, your messenger showed up with the news of his death."

"I don't suppose she also told you she sicced the cops on me on the subsequent evening?"

"Wouldn't surprise me. That's the reason she came here, Lloyd. To make known in no uncertain terms that she wants you to take the fall. Even if you're cleared of his death, she intends to do you dirt in retaliation for, what I'm guessing is some sort of slight on your part."

Brick shakes his head ruefully,"She's got nothin'."

"Might not matter that much Lloyd, if she's serious about it. The widow of a decorated ex-police detective can make some noise, even if it turns out he was a louse."

Brick looks down and nods thoughtfully,"Yeah, I get it. All the more reason for me to wrap this all up as tidy as possible." He turns and crosses to the door, "Thanks, Clarence."

"Don't mention it. To anybody."

Brick nods in acquiescence and exits.

Brick returns to the taxicab and as he approaches, the driver springs out and holds the door open for him. Brick starts at this show of what is usually regarded as male etiquette, but responds with an amused smile,"Thanks."

"My pleasure!" She trills as she scampers back and slides behind the wheel. At 3:01 they pull into the shadow cast by the dome of city hall. After he finishes with the recompense for her services, plus a generous tip, she hands him her business card with her contact information,"In case you need a top-notch wheelman", she explains. "And I can reach you at this number, day or night?" He asks. "Sure", she responds. "But, nights are better, I work days." And with a wink she pulls away from the curb.

Brick enters the door with the number 322 painted on the glass and is immediately met by a scaled down version of the District Attorney himself, down to the prince nez and hair part in the middle of his squat skull. He is led to an inner office door, with a brass name plate: Bryan Monahan. The miniature opens the door, and closes it behind Lloyd as the D.A. himself rises and offers Lloyd a stout but well manicured hand.

"Mr. District Attorney."

"Oh, Bryan, please, Lloyd. Just friends here." After clasping Brick's hand in his own to shake he releases one to gesture for his midget self to take Brick's hat and coat which he does and hangs them on an elaborate rack which includes a gilt edged mirror and elephant's foot umbrella stand. As the young attendant exits, closing the door behind him, Monahan offers Brick a seat which he accepts. The official crosses to a wet bar and asks, "Bourbon fine?"

"Great."

While the libation is being prepared, Brick scans the office, taking in the deep leather furniture and polished brass and walnut wood paneling. Monahan brings Brick his drink, hands it to him and taps the rim of their tumblers together: "To your good health," he says with a smile that doesn't quite reach his eyes.

"Prost." Brick replies and takes a small taste. Two fingers of very good bourbon whiskey. He takes another sip and looks around the room again and offers amiably,"A drink, no stenographer, no A.D.A's. To what do I owe this informality?"

Monanhan sits on the edge of his desk and the smile becomes a little broader. "Our respective roles have sometimes seen us on opposite ends of an issue, but we do have deep and abiding interests in common. We're not ones for small talk and we both have a great regard and affection for our magnificent city."

Already Brick can tell a grand bargain is in the offing, but so far nothing he can refute. He sips and waits for the approach and the contingencies. What chink in his armor was about to be exploited?

"Your partner," the D.A. purses his already thin lips and shakes his conical head. "A police veteran with a trenchant reputation as a proponent of law and order." He sighs and casts his gaze somewhere towards the ceiling. "Unsolved violence such as this wounds the whole body politic. It is incumbent upon us the resolve this as quickly and as efficiently as possible."

"Of course," thinks Brick. "Use the dead man. It's the path of least resistance." He swirls his drink and offers in an off-hand way,"You could already have had that. Just give Maclane his head and you'll have mine and quite a tidy little package."

The bespectacled man almost winces and turns his attention back to Brick,"I wish you wouldn't regard this little get-together as adversarial. And please don't think I've any belief – much less confidence – in those theories the police have been formulating."

"That sounds reassuring."

"Don't misunderstand me, Lloyd – I may call you Lloyd?" He looks down into his drink."Our initial request was in the interest of making sure that your firm's activities were compliant with all existing-"

"Then rumors of a Fed probe into certain extra curricular activities during war time are true, then?" Brick's tone makes this a statement rather than a question.

The District Attorney clears his throat uncomfortably and frowns, "There are things that may still resonate after Walter Diamond's demise and it would be a terrible shame if anything were come to light that might unfairly diminish the stature of any of those who may have close to him."

"My late partner was rather ubiquitous in his dealings. That circle could probably fill a good size ballroom."

"Precisely," the D.A. beams as hops off of the desk and makes his way around to the chair and sits. He clasps the arm rest of his oversized leather chair and rocks back comfortably,"To keep such an unfortunate circumstance from occurring, this office is prepared to assist you in assuring that justice is, from this point on, administered with swiftness and thoroughness." The lenses of his glasses catch the light and mask his eyes from view.

"Very generous," Brick sips, holds the glass out a little and admires the color,"You may not be much on small talk, but your way with ambiguity makes your meaning loud and clear. And just what might that offer entail from my end to keep me from such guilt by association?"

"I'm glad you seems so amenable." He leans forwards and says in a hushed tone,"We have managed to secure an audience for you with – The Colonel." His stare glitters with expectancy. Brick stares back. Then,"Teddy Roosevelt's been gone almost three decades now, so I'm sure I -"

"Oh, very droll – no, I was referring to Colonel Casper; a very old, old patron of the city. He has endowed many institutions in the bay area with his philanthropy."

"Really? How come I'm not familiar with him if he's such a prominent benefactor to our fair city?"

Monahan turns the chair and rises from his seat and begins to pace the room, hands behind his back addressing the general air:"The Colonel has been abroad for many of the last few years. His.... interests keep him almost constantly on the move. Besides being transient, there are matters of his health as well...." for this he turns to face Brick,"Part of his seclusion is that he requires very special surroundings in order to not exacerbate his condition."

"Which is?"

He shrugs and cocks his head to one side as he winds his way back towards his desk,"I don't know. And I don't know that anyone does. He was in his late fifties when he went to Egypt over two decades ago and disappeared. When he was found again a few years later, it was obvious that what ever happened, he returned from the ordeal a changed man."

"And the Colonel will set my feet on the right path?"

"The Colonel has resources and.... wisdom that can hardly be equaled. I'm sure once he's explained things – you're an erudite and worldly individual – you'll understand the implications and see your way clear to help in the inoculation of the city from unjust and unwarranted entanglements."

Brick smiles to himself and downs the last of his drink. He stands and thumps it down on the desktop and heads for the coat rack,"Both you and the police seem to think you've got me over a barrel. If I come in with you, you'll always feel you can bring me to heel whenever the biggest dog barks." He lifts his coat from the rack and folds it over one arm and reaches for his hat.

"As far as I can see, the best chance I have of clearing myself of the trouble that someone is trying to make for me is by reeling the whole thing in – all tied up. And my only chance of catching the responsible parties and bringing them to answer for what they've done is by keeping away from you and the police, because neither of you show any signs of knowing what the hell it's all about." And with that, he abruptly places his hat on his head and opens the door. "See you at the inquest, maybe." And with that he exits and slams the door behind him.

Monahan frowns after him. Then the District Attorney puts his finger on one of the pearl buttons in a battery of four on his desk and speaks into the intercom:"Plan B. Get me the marina."

Brick rides down from the third floor in an elevator. His lips are dry and he tries, but fails to work up the saliva to moisten them. Then he realizes his heart is hammering in his jaw and his eyes sting from perspiration trickling down from under his hat band. When he takes out his handkerchief to wipe his face he sees his hand trembling. He grins at it and exhales so loudly that the elevator-operator turns his head and glares.

Brick sits in a booth at John's Grill fifteen minutes later, toying with a water glass as he waits for his order. He is glad he dismissed the young lady driver earlier and caught a cabbie he didn't know. He feels somehow he wouldn't want her to be cognizant of his current state of mind. In the back of the cab, the previous passenger left behind a section of the newspaper turned to his ex-partner's case. He glanced at it – enough to catch the drift: brutal crime, many leads, no results, the see-saw of apportionment of blame.

Now, for the fifth time since he was seated – an old customer (Nothing too good for, Mr. Brick!) - he removes a small, round tin container from his suit coat pocket and absently, but gently shakes it, making an accompaniment to the erratic sparking of his thoughts. He cranes his neck to see if the waitress is coming and spies the angular frame of Louis Pines hovering near the door. He abruptly ducks back. Then chances another discreet glance – sure Pines wasn't even been looking in his direction.

This time all he sees is the backs of two local congressmen who, conjoined at the shoulders, are weaving their way to the entrance. Brick's eyes flicker around the immediate area. Nothing. He starts to sit back when he is startled by the approach of Senor Terranova. Brick yelps in surprise and throws up an arm to possibly defend himself. The little tin box clatters on the tabletop.

"Cripes! You OK, Mr. Brick? I'm didn't meanta startle ya."

Brick sits back, breathing rapidly as he stares at the wisps of hair across the gleaning dome, like sad seaweed stranded by the tide. His gaze drops further to the anxious eyes and gaping maw of Claude Fry, one of the resident barkeeps. Brick wipes his hands on his thighs and nods at the sturdy figure,"Sorry, Claude. Nerves is all."

"Don't know as I'd blame ya. What with Walt getting' aired out like that. Here, this should be just the tonic."

He takes the glass from the trey he is holding and serves it to Brick. He reaches for the glass already on the table,"Water back?" Brick snatches the pill box back and fumbles in his pants pocket, pulls a couple of crumpled bills out and tosses them onto the tray and dismisses his waiter,"Uh, no. No thanks, kid." The bartender eyes Brick, taking in his somewhat rattled behavior, but fishes the bills off of the trey and retreats,"Sure thing, Mr. B."

Brick waits until the coast is clear and pulls out the tin receptacle again. He tries to open the lid, but jittery fingers lose their grip and the bright yellow ellipses skitter across the tabletop. His hands clap the box together and shove it down next to his side. He reaches out a scoops the pills back towards his edge of the table, all the while keeping a lookout to see if his fumbling had been observed. He is tempted to scoop a handful of pills at a time, then stops. He tosses them in his hands a couple of times then takes a breath and tips his hand and pours them all back into the tin, except one. He takes the one pill and picks up the glass that had been served to him and downs it in one shot. He sets the glass down on the table with a satisfied,"Ahh...." and exhales. He feels the vodka fumes scald his membranes and rises from the table and exits.

Lorna Christie is standing in the middle of the outer office when he entered. She looks at him with urgent brown eyes and asks,"What happened?"

Brick stops dead in his tracks,"What happened, what?"

"12C: what happened?"

"What are you telling me?" He crosses to her and grabs her upper arms.

"I went to the hotel, like you said, already to pack her up and bring her back here if necessary, but by the time I got there she was gone," she wails.

"Gahh!" He yells and releases her, throwing his hands in the air and shaking his head as he stalks about the room.

Lorna offers,"Somebody must have followed her."

He stops moving long enough to say,"Pines was in the lobby when I left, but I tailed him to Alameda. Maybe Terranova, maybe.... I don't know!" He throws his hands in the air again in disgust. Then he turns back to Lorna,"Did you try your switchboard grapevine?"

She rubs her arms where his hands had been,"Of course. Nothing's turned up so far."

He returns to grumbling and starts smacking one fist into the other as he stalks, Lorna watches him with wary eyes. Finally he stops moving, places his hands on his hips as his head drops back and he gazes at the ceiling with an exasperated sigh,"I'm going out and find her if I have to scour the sewers. Wait here til I get back or you here from me. For Christ's sake let's do something right."

He starts for the door and opens it, but before he exits he leans in and says,"You know better than to pay attention to me when I talk like that, right?

She snorts and her mouth twitches,"God-damned schoolboy. I won't be able to wear an evening gown for two weeks." She continues rubbing her shoulders and pouting.

He shrugs and admits,"I'm just no damned good." He is about to back out of the office when his egress is impeded. A dark, imposing figure stumbles against him and pushes them both back into the office.

"Hey! What the -?" Brick manages to separate himself from the other body as it staggers towards the middle of the room and turns,"You know -" is all it manages to get out along with a bubbling froth of blood that spatters from it's lips. A black overcoat topped with a black bowler hat, the figure starts to sway. Brick recognizes him from his audience with Man Fat; the bodyguard. Held tight against the left side of his barrel chest by a black-sleeved arm is a paper-wrapped parcel bound with thin rope - an ellipsoid a little larger than an American football.

Lorna bites the knuckle of her forefinger to keep from screaming as the stout Japanese puts both hands over his bundle and with a last gurgling rattle falls forward like a felled tree, flat on his face. Or he would have if Brick hadn't stepped in and to catch him. The man sags at the knees and the object he is holding drops with a resounding thud and rolls away from them. Brick slowly lowers the body to the floor where the very last breath seems to wheeze out. Brick turns to Lorna and whispers urgently,"Lock the door!"

Lorna starts and hurries to the door, closes it firmly with both hands then leans on the door with her shoulder as she locks it. Brick manages to extricate his hands from the man long enough to register the blood on them. With what fingers has has left unblemished, he gingerly unbuttons the top coat and reveals the blood sodden suit coat underneath. His ponderous torso was ragged with holes. Still leaning on the door, Lorna asks," Is – is he -?"

Brick raises himself up on knee at a time, but keeps his eyes on the prone figure,"Yeah. Shot through the chest maybe half a dozen times. At least he didn't get it in the back." He crosses to the washbowl in the outer office and begins to wash his hands. "Who is he? Do you know?" Lorna crosses to the body and leans a little closer to examine his face.

"Yeah. A Tong supernumerary. Why did he come here? He couldn't have come far with those holes in him."

Lorna spies the bundle which rolled away under one of the guest chairs. She straightens up and points to it as Brick emerges from the restroom, drying his hands with a towel,"Maybe that will tell us," she says. Brick crosses to it and scoops it up from the floor and carries it to her desk. He sets it down with the knotted side up. He tries to untangle the knots but they are hard and tight. Lorna reaches into the top drawer of her desk and pulls out a pocket knife which she hands to Brick. He smiles at her, wipes his hands on his trousers and takes the knife and cuts the rope.

Lorna leans over his shoulder, her voice tight with excitement,"Do you think it is?"

"We'll soon know,"Brick says as his fingers peel away first one layer of packaging and then another. He gets to thin layer of straw and once through that they were left with an egg shaped, pale wadding of excelsior. Brick stops and glances at his secretary/partner who glances back. They are both breathing hard. He plunges fingers of both hands into the wadding and pulls it apart revealing a lightly mottled ceramic container, about a foot or so high, with a lid formed in the head of a creature with an angular snout and sharp, pointed ears.

Brick lifts it up, brushing packing remnants from it. He turns it over in his hands, holding it up to the light.

"Is that it? Really the one?"

"I don't know," Brick says as he lowers it and sets it on the desk top where they can both regard it. "Remind me, partner to be kind to the next encyclopedia salesman who comes calling."

"Maybe I should call the Professor to verify -"

Just then the phone rings and they both turn the heads. After the second ring they look to each other. He nods and she picks up the receiver and says,"Hello... Yes... Who?... Oh, yes!" She covers the mouthpiece and is about to call Brick to the phone when a shriek comes over the receiver that even Brick can hear. Lorna puts the receiver back up to her ear,"Hello? Hello!"She rattles the cradle prong up and down and cries again,"Hello! Hello!" Brick moves quickly to her side as she hangs up. "It was Miss Markov, Lloyd. She sounded desperate – her voice was terrible. Something happened to her before she could finish!" She is clutching at Brick now. "She needs you. You've got to go help her, Lloyd!"

"You realize that leaves you to deal with this?" He gestures to the body, now leaking crimson on the floor. "We've got the object of desire. That means we're in the driver's seat. I'm taking this with me for safekeeping." He starts to repackage the jar.

"You just get a move on. We've seen the price in human life they place on this thing. I'll call this in,"Lorna says in a small voice.

"OK, just tell it like it happened, but leave out the part about the parcel. Oh, and I got the call, not you. Wish I knew where I was going", Brick mutters. They manage to re-conceal the container, although the packaging is less homogenous than before.

"Don't you have any idea where she might – oh wait, I remember something...." She frowns in concentration:"In the background, there was noise, wind maybe and – and a bell...."

"Like a buoy, maybe?"

She starts from her reverie eagerly,"Maybe!"

He shrugs into his coat, places his hat on his head, grabs the package, tucks it under one arm and crosses to the door. Lorna follows him. "Lock the door behind me." He reaches out and taps her on the chin with his fist,"You're a damned good man, sister." And with that he backs out the door.

Carrying the parcel he retraces his route from his first foray into this diabolical venture. Hailing a taxicab from the corner of Kearny and Post Streets just outside the narrow courtyard behind his office building, he instructs the driver to take them to Fifth Street, all the while constantly checking his surroundings. He has the cabbie drop him in front of the Pickwick Stage terminal, where he checks the package into the Parcel

Room, inserts the check into an envelope which he addresses with the name N. Charles and a San Francisco post office box number, seals it and drops it in the mail box.

Brick drops a dime at the nearest phone booth and fishes a card out of his breast pocket. Twelve minutes later, the brunette taxicab driver comes to a screeching stop in front of Brick as he stands by the curb near Fifth and Howard.

As he climbs in she asks,"Business or pleasure?"

"Old Alameda Point and yesterday."

She drops him off by a copse of trees several dozen yards away from the boat ramp. It is twilight. Shreds of fog swell and swirl, shrouding light and vision. Brick strides quickly towards the ship's berth avoiding the pink and amber spill of overhead lights along the waterway. He sees no one. Not even in the distance. The quay likewise seems deserted, and the gangplank bumps gently in the swell. The sun is properly down now and the last of the day's warmth seems to have dissipated like the light.

He treads as lightly as possible up the gangplank. His breath steams in the light drizzle that wafts from the sea in viscid drafts of air. He sees light from portholes above and decides to head for the midship house. He slips quickly and quietly up to the boat deck. He crouches and slides to the side of one of the portholes and looks in. Darya, in a green dress pacing, talking to someone he cannot see from his angle. She seems animated; gesticulating and running her hand through her hair. He is about to work his way to another porthole when he is taken from behind by powerful arms. He can feel the one hand griping the back of his head and forcing it into the elbow crook of the other arm. He struggles, but is lifted off of his feet. He becomes cognizant of a musky odor which he at first mistakes for Terranova's scent, but is muskier.

Brick manages to hook one foot behind one of assailant's knees and starts to twist free when another powerful grip seizes him by his coat front and pulls him back down to the deck. Brick can smell him before he sees him: Terranova. Clawing at the arm that is smothering him he can just make out the cracked, sneering visage of the stout little Latin. His vision starts to swim and darkness closes in on the edges. "Well, at least I wasn't hit in the head", is all that comes to mind as he loses consciousness.

8

Swell Lot O' Thieves

"Are you pretending, is this the ending unless I can have one more chance to prove dear? My life a wreck your making, you know I'm yours just for the taking. I'd gladly surrender body and soul...."

These lyrics burble through Brick's ears. Blackness becomes mottled with shades of gray and then muted colors. His eyes open. He is staring at a white bulkhead. He turns his head towards the sound of the voice and his focus comes to rest on a stalactite of flaxen locks, swaying softly beside the bunk he is lying on. His movement must have alerted the siren, because her song now ceases.

A shadow shrouded face looms over him, the light from the overhead globe casts an aureole around the pale helmet of hair that now drapes over him. A husky voice declares,"You're awake." The head withdraws after a moment, leaving a tingle of delicate scent lingering over him. He slowly sits up, holding onto the side of the bunk. He looks up to see: eyes narrow and hazel, cheek bones you could open bottle caps under.

"How long have I -"

"Not long", she says in weary tone. "Here," she wrings out a washcloth in the sink stand next to her and presses him back down and places the moistened fabric on his forehead. Brick allows himself the luxury of her ministrations and decides to seek her as an avenue of information.

"Feels like we're underway."

"Mm", she assents as she turns to the desk next to the bunk. The lid has been lowered to allow access and to provide a work surface. On the desk there is a Waterford crystal brandy decanter with two matching glasses. One is obviously already in use. She sits in the chair she has pulled up next to the bunk and retrieves her glass and drinks,"About time. Damned fog…." She shudders, then lounges back indolently in a tight fitting striped top with sequins and harem pants. One knee crosses over the other, and a restless sandal-ed foot bounces as she sips at her drink.

Brick realizes that the convalescent approach will only take him so far with the present company, so he slides the cloth off of his head, locks his eyes on hers and sits up. Never releasing her gaze, he swings his legs over and settles his feet on the floor. In this narrow berth, that makes for some intimacy. He glances to the desk and back,"Aren't you going to offer me one? Medicinal purposes and all."

"What does my father want to see you for?"

"Your father? Oh, you must mean the Colonel. Is that why the nocturnal cruise?"

"I guess. Wish he'd waited until tomorrow, when the sun is up." She shivers again, and sips. Her forehead is wide and her eyebrows are sublime wings which hover over her gaze which never leaves him. She quiets her foot and shifts herself slightly in her seat to accommodate him, moving her legs past his. Their knees graze each other.

"So, your a shamus. Not quite what I expected. I thought they only existed in cheap magazines and dime-store novels or else were grubby little window peepers."

"I'll take that as a complement, back-handed or otherwise. And what about that drink? Or did that sound too grubby?"

She snorts, but he's not sure if it is from laughter or not. He feels her foot trace lightly up his shin as she rises and moves to the other side of the wash stand. She leans against the bulkhead, one arm across her waist the other elbow tucked into her upturned palm, the hand holding her drink aloft. "Get it yourself", she snaps in a low, vexed tone.

He shrugs and rises. The decanter is now in arm's reach and he lifts it, opens it and pours about two fingers worth into his glass. He holds the drink up in a brief toast which she acknowledges with a nod and he drinks.

The liquid is thick and heady. He exhales with a small 'Whoosh' and turns the glass in his hand and eyeball's the contents.

Her mouth twitches and the semblance of dimples appear,"Croizet cognac, 1892."

"From what little I've heard about the Colonel, I suppose I shouldn't expect anything less."

"If it's information about my father that you're hoping to pry from me, I'm afraid you'd be wasting much of your time." She looks at her drink closely.

"Consider yourself a hard case, do you?"

Something between a pout and a sigh escapes her. Then,"My father disappeared from my life before I was five years old. He was never much of a father even when he was around, always off somewhere obsessed with the past which didn't leave me with much of a future after my mother died."

She lets the hand with the drink drop to her side."I was schooled abroad, never really knew my home or family. My mother died when I was a year old, I was basically raised by a trust." She takes a drink and turns to Brick,"Then nine years ago, two large, dark men basically kidnapped me from my school in Switzerland and I've been on the seven seas ever since."

"At your father's insistence, I take it. You his daughter or his prisoner?"

Her face darkens and crumbles,"I don't have many childhood memories of my father, but he's.... not exactly what I remember. His interest in me is purely.... ancestoral."

Brick downs the rest of his drink and winces at the after-taste."Nine years. Many ports of call. The life of a brigand must agree with you. That must explain the expensive grog intake."

The temperature in the cabin plummets as she drops both of her hands to her sides,"I don't like your manners. People don't talk to me like that."

"I don't care if you like my manners, I've been bushwhacked and ambushed and treated like a punching bag by every one who has a stake in this lunatic pursuit so pardon me if I don't grieve over my social shortcomings while I'm being shanghaied."

She continues to glare at him, then drops her head and whispers,"If you only knew...." Then she abruptly crosses to him, sets her glass on the desktop and reaches up and grabs his lapel with one hand while the other comes to rest on his breast. She looks searchingly up into his eyes,"If you make it out of here alive, take me with you." She turns her body and her hip slides along his flank.

Brick is taken aback and before he can respond, the hatch to the cabin scrapes open and they look up to see: Darya. She stands poised in the doorway, taking in the seemingly intimate scene before her with aplomb. Brick's nursemaid drops her gaze and sways away from him and picks up her drink. As she slinks to the hatchway, Darya merely watches her with a slightly quizzical air. Just before Brick's caretaker slips out the door she turns provocatively in the open hatchway,"Oh, and if you should need any little old thing, all you have to do is whistle…. just whistle." And with that she languorously takes her leave.

Brick and his client regard each other in silence. She is dressed in a tan coat with pleats and a green leaf emblem embroidered on one lapel in a green to match the blouse underneath. Finally, she tosses her head slightly and with a small smile moves slowly towards him,"You're a mess, aren't you?"

"You, on the other hand, don't seem the worse for wear," he responds evenly.

She stops and looks down,"I'm sorry, I – I had no choice." Her hands work anxiously at her sides. Then she rushes to Brick and embraces him, her head on his chest,"Oh, Lloyd. Let's get out of here, just the two of us."

"If we get much further out, I'm not sure anyone is getting out of here. Alive."

"Do you really think they'll -"

"Once they have the dingus there won't be much of a hand left to play…."

"There are two lifeboats. I'm sure we could get to one of them. There aren't more than a dozen people in the crew."

"Suddenly, every woman I meet wants to do a duet on the lam." He holds her out at arm's length, "And suddenly, you're a font of information. Well, we're sitting on dynamite and who knows how long before the powers that be might decide to lose some dangerous ballast."

"Are you sure you didn't just get a better offer?" she says with wounded eyes.

"She's everything I need in the world, but she doesn't strike sparks. And where would we go? And what would we use to get there? No. When your partner's killed you're supposed to do something about it. It doesn't matter what you thought of him, it's something that can't be allowed to be gotten away with. Not in a life or death business like ours. I intend to make it back to my city alive and that I can go with my head held high. Or at least make sure they're very sorry they ever saw me."

Brick watches her struggle as her eyes flicker and probe his. She swallows and says,"I – I'll tell you all I can."

"Could the Colonel be the one who hired you to go to Pearl Harbor?"

"I – I don't know. I suppose. But, I've never met him before tonight."

"Pines and Terranova are on board. Are they working for the Colonel, too?"

"I don't know about Senor Terranova, but Pines found me and made me make that telephone call and brought me here."

"So, Terranova interferes with your orders in Hawaii. Follows you to San Francisco, but doesn't find himself any closer to his objective and is now seemingly in cahoots with the Colonel." He massages an earlobe while pacing. He stops and muses. "And it three days before yous how up about Pines..." He stops and places his hands on his hips."It seems as if things have been steered to this point."

She looks at him eagerly,"What do you think they have in mind?"

"All the major players seem to be aboard except for...." He turns and looks pointedly at her.

"Well, that may be, but that doesn't mean I know anything about – all I know is that I was offered ten thousand dollars to get the jar and leave it at a drop to be specified later and then...." She trails off with a despairing gesture.

In the background the moan of a fog horn lends a throb to the night air that cuts through the hiss of the wind and waves. Brick turns towards the porthole,"We must be passing the Gate." They both cross to the opening and through the mist encrusted glass they see the bridge, looming in the dark. A ghostly cathedral for giants.

They both turn from the bulkhead and to each other. Brick,"Unless your side is willing to up the stakes, I'd say it's the Colonel's hand to play. And mine, at least until I decide to turn over the trinket."

Darya's face pales with surprise,"You? You have....how...?"

Brick,"Seemingly a gift from Man Fat, but I wonder…." He smacks one fist against the other as he paces to the porthole. "Considering the extraordinary abilities and apparent resources of our hosts. It may have gotten to the point where the only recourse is to heave a wild and unpredictable monkey wrench into the machinery. If only I could find out more about Terranova and the -"

"He's a gnome," comes an unexpected voice. Darya gasps and they both look up to see the ponderous head of Man Fat looming in the porthole.

"Gnome abilities vary", he continues genially. "But, their one common trait is acquisitiveness. Principally precious stones and metal. Originally from the Iberian peninsula, Senor Augusto Terranova is an earth spirit."

The hatch to the cabin creaks open, Terranova steps in with a gun in his hand trained on Brick. He leans casually against the frame. The cold night air flutters the loose ends of his too long scarf.

"That oaky, woody scent that even the smell of cyphre can't quite cover up," Brick muses.

Man Fat,"Precisely." And with that he appears in the doorway. Terranova rolls aside as the gargantuan counterfeit Asian maneuvers his bulk into the cabin by sections. Once inside the pair make for an almost comical sight in the disparity of their scale. But, Brick is not in a laughing mood.

"The rich volcanic earth in Hawaii keeps him 'young'. And he's been an invaluable resource for us there." Man Fat says as he beams cheerfully down at his cohort.

"Too much rain," the rotund figure grumbles.

"Our paths crossed a few years back in the pursuit of a rare relic from the Crusades in Constantinople. He's always preferred more moderate climes." He seems about to pat his short compatriot on the head, then thinks better of it and strokes his own mustache.

"I noticed he has a tendency to go all to pieces when the weather gets a little soggy," Brick smirks.

"An irony I'm sure you have noticed when you consider our current mode of transport. But, he's not the only one who requires a more arid environment,"Man Fat says. "This vessel is not only unique in and of itself, but the same could be said for many aboard her." He looks pointedly at Darya.

"That must explain the overgrown snow globe aft." Brick says as he nods in the direction of the rear of the ship.

Man Fat's mouth curls in appreciation,"Indeed. In fact I've been sent to invite you to the captain's table, as it were, for dinner. Until such time we will leave you to your own devices, but be warned, any attempt at escape will be considered an extreme affront to our host. In the meantime I'm sure your alluring client can keep you entertained, after all she is descendant from Eden before the fall. That should provide many possible topics for discourse."

Brick looks at Darya quizzically, but she keeps her eyes fixed on the other two as they move to effect their exit.

"Come, Senor. Let us leave the detective and his client alone. I am sure they have much to discuss regarding certain privileges," Man Fat says breezily. "Oh, and the Colonel has a late supper planned, I hear. And we have been instructed to dress appropriately". His eyes scale up and down Brick critically. Then he turns and ducks his bulk through the hatchway. Terranova smirks and clangs the hatch shut behind him. The noise chills Brick as if it were a gate in the slammer. Darya remains silent. The wind whistles in shrilly bursts outside and the ship rolls with the dark cold swell. When she finally turns to Brick, her eyes are as iridescent as peacock feathers.

Brick looks quickly away, tugs at an earlobe and begins to pace back and forth,"The Biblical reference is a little arcane for me, but considering the unique nature of the other players involved, I should've been more skeptical of your own abilities." He stops in front of her,"All you needed was to put your lovely painted nail on the scale and I'd be sure to turn the beam in your favor."

Her eyes flick down, but he holds his gaze steady on her face.

"I can more than guess at what you special 'gift' is. You took even took me to bed to keep me from asking questions -"

Darya starts at this and clasps his arms,"Oh, Lloyd. How can you say such a thing when – why darling, I knew from the moment I walked in your office –"

Brick,"I won't follow in I don't know how many others footsteps. Have you ever given me truth or confidence? Are you still just hoping it all comes out right? Still hoping to get your hands on it in the end? And for whom?"

Her eyes flash as he grasps her hard by the shoulders, his jaw clenched, his mouth a taut grimace of resolve. Then, they both start and glance to the hatchway as the screech of metal on metal announces the entrance of -

Louis Pines. His rawboned frame dangling in the hatchway like a demented scarecrow as he leers at the couple, "The Colonel requests a business conference with the – gentleman."

Brick and Darya exchange glances. He releases her and nods at Pines and gathers his hat and coat. He shrugs on his coat and Pines retreats outside as he hits the exit.

"You're still the client. Any instructions?" he offers as he stands at the hatchway.

She opens her mouth to reply, then thinks better of it.

Brick nods and gestures for Pines to lead the way. Pines smirks and turns his back on Brick and saunters ahead, his hands casually resting in the pockets of his trench coat. He leads them aft and they descend to the deck level to where the vast, vaulted glass and metal conservatory of Victorian style and symmetry looms over them. Where one would expect a hatch cover, a small atrium enclosure looms. Pines opens the exterior doors and gesture for Brick to enter. After, they are both in, Pines moves past Brick to another set of doors set in further by another twelve feet.

He opens the one on the right and gestures for Brick to enter. He does so and is immediately assaulted by an almost smothering heat. Except for half a dozen lamps burning high in the rafter above them, the space is illuminated only by a few cast iron heaters with electric coils and three braziers whose open flames causing shadows to dance and prank. He casts his gaze about and finds the area is fringed with some rather bedraggled looking palm trees while the majority of the area is laid out with large beds of undulating sand dotted with a variety of cacti.

From nearby he hears would could be murmuring voices. Pines sidles up beside him and nods for Brick to advance. Brick frowns, but accedes. As he slowly moves forward the sounds take on a more urgent and plaintive nature. They seem to be coming from a small copse of palm trees with smaller potted palms screening it. As he steps closer he recognizes his nursemaid from before. She seems to be squirming in the grasp of someone seated. Brick catches her white, livid face; it looks pinched, drained, but her eyes flare as she finally wrenches free from the grasp of someone seated just beyond Brick's vantage point.

Brick feels Pines close in behind his shoulder. His breath comes in huffs, right over Brick's collar. Brick glances up to catch Pines' expression: strained, his yellow eyes glittering with suppressed emotion, his upper lip drawing up into a sneer. Brick turns back to the plight of the Colonel's daughter just as Pines brushes past him into the intimate scene. The daughter starts with surprise at his abrupt appearance, then rubbing the wrist she broke free from the seated figure, she suddenly bolts out of the plants and across Brick's path. She again seems startled seeing him, then she turns her face away and stumbles off in the direction of the doors. Brick gestures after her, but Pines' voice rasps out behind him,"OK. The Colonel will see you now."

Brick turns and brushes through the foliage. As he approaches the seated figure he removes his hat and looks up to see –

A wavering knob of a head, a discolored handkerchief clutched to it's mouth and nose by a spindly hand over which two sunken orbs glitter. He coughs and crumples the linen in his hand, but not fast enough to keep Brick from catching the dark, viscous liquid within.

"How do you feel about succulents?" comes a voice, although rattling with age still delivered with command.

Brick,"Carefully."

The old man doesn't seem to acknowledge the jest. He extends a palsied and spindly hand and brushes at the nearest specimen,"Cactus. Ugly, brutal, fascinating things." He withdraws his hand, bearing a scarab ring, Brick notices. After a moment offers in a wily voice,"Much like myself, you're not doubt thinking." And with that he rolls slowly forward revealing a unique mechanized wheelchair in which the frangible frame of the Colonel leaned, swathed in an ocher colored thobe overlaid with an earth-colored kibr and a burgundy aba.

He wears a skullcap that only serves to accentuate his cadaverous appearance. The skull itself is a battered asteroid. The eyes are deep-set, dark and liquid, unwavering in their gaze which is now locked on Brick. The sclera is yellow with age, but the sharp intent in their gaze holds firm.

His skin recedes from a prominent nose like a series of salt flats - a scaly and rutted topography. His clipped vocal cadence hints at middle-eastern origins.

Colonel,"You are looking at a very dull survival of a rather adventurous and accomplished life. If not for the accident, the fire in my tent, disease, laid up for so long, in-contactable...."He waves his thin hand in a vague gesture of blessing or dismissal. He leans forward and his eyes and voice narrow,"Carter and Herbert found Tut and were glorified. My find could not be proclaimed, yet. But, it will change everything."

Brick almost expects him to cackle malevolently, but the elderly explorer looks sharply at him, pats the arms of the chair and says animatedly,"Always been quite the inventor. Designed this ship, too." He cranes his neck around slowly, his gaze indicating the glass enclosure. "Cactus is excuse for the dry heat. At my age, moisture could lead to serious infection. Compromise immune system. Irony of being on the ocean.... salt at least. The old man's focus returns to Brick,"You may remove your jacket and tie for your comfort, sir. This place is too stifling for anyone that has any blood in them."

"Thanks," Brick responds gratefully as he removes his jacket and loosens his tie and collar. His host gestures to someone beyond Brick's view. After draping his jacket over the back of the chair he resumes his seat as Pines moves closer to the back of his chair. The henchman is still attired in his hat and trench coat.

"The duties of a domestic seems a little incongruous with the perpetual five o'clock shadow,"Brick says as he jerks his thumb at the gangly gunsel.

Yellow eyes flash as Pine's hands thrust into his pockets as he steps slowly forward,"Remember, I warned you guys about how you talk -"

The Colonel raises a palm of censure at his servant, but addresses Brick,"Are you attempting to tell him his duties, sir?"

Brick,"No, just having fun trying to guess what they are," he says lightly.

Pines growls,"Why are we dealing with him?" but, he stops his advance.

Brick smiles slightly,"Possession is nine-tenth's of the negotiation, mutt."

Pines snaps,"Keep it up and I'm gonna be pickin' your liver out of my teeth."

Brick coolly responds,"Present company included, I'll take that as a distinct possibility, but better ask your boss if he wants me to be an hors d'oeuvre before we start."

Colonel,"Now, Louis that's enough of that. Get the detective a drink." He scowls and flaps a thin, dismissive hand at the sullen minion.

Brick can feel Pines bristle in response, but after a moment he turns abruptly and exits. Brick believes he hears more grumbling as Pines weaves his way carefully through the nettlesome foliage.

Colonel,"There were Primitives even on this land even before it was a continent. He's always affected a New Jersey affectation." He shrugs,"Although I did first run into him not far south of Philadelphia some years back." The old man absently scratches at the withered wattle dangling from his throat.

Brick,"Never mind the rouge's gallery of Fairytale Town,"Brick says bluntly. "Let's talk about the bat."

The thin man abruptly ceases his scraping and looks at Brick. He lowers his hand as his eyes narrow. He nods his head slowly,"All right, sir," he agreed. "Let's." He screws up his eyes and asks,"I believe our erstwhile Asian has indicated that you had found some credence to his history?"

Brick,"That's a moot point. I've gotten to know what value in human life you all seem to place on it."

The Colonel's eye-lids draw down,"Then you must also have an inkling of where you stand in the negotiations."

Brick leans back and responds evenly,"You want the bat. I've got it. A fall-guy is part of the price I'm asking. And a quarter of what your realize on the article."

At this the Colonel's face actually seems to animate with something like surprise,"By Gad sir, the blustering behemoth is right; you are a character!" He steeples his thin fingers together and they take on a pulsing motion,"They said there's never any telling what you'll do or say next, except that it's bound to be something startling." After perusing him thoughtfully for a moment, he folds his fingers together and drops his hands into his lap,"Not that I wasn't prepared for your expression of self-interest, but that you could so readily obviate such a compelling client as Miss Markov...."

Brick smiles thinly,"Don't be too sure I'm as high-minded as I'm supposed to be. After all, it's not as if my partner's proclivities were unknown to me nor their relative benefits."

The Colonel's smile replicates Brick's in it's leanness,"A reputation that might attract the most lucrative clients and make it easier to deal with the adversary."

Brick merely stretches his tight smile in acquiescence. A silence as thick as salt water taffy pulls between them. Finally, the Colonel gives a little shrug,"Well, sir, if you're really serious about this, the least I can do in common politeness is to hear you out. We do have refreshments coming and in the meantime the interval is yours to beguile." He gesture generously if shakily. "Now mind you, I don't see how this suggestion of yours is in any way practical - ", he leans in slightly,"It would seem that the authorities in your city

Brick,"Not at all. Monahan is like most district attorneys. He's more interested in how his record looks in the papers than in anything else. In fact, I'm doing his work for him by coming up with a clear cut case for conviction, rather than trying to shepherd a tangled web of characters and their seemingly supernatural inclinations and murky associations through the court."

Just then, a clattering sound causes both men to look up to see –

Pines returning, wheeling a portable bar which he brings to a sudden, tinkling halt. Both men watch as the surly server mixes brandy and champagne from a towel-swathed ice bucket into two crystal flutes. He hands them to the seated gentlemen and the elder of the two holds his up to the dim light,"As cold as the desert stars...." Then he nods to his guest,"To your very good health, sir. And a profitable accord for all."

Brick nods in assent and drinks. The cold and fermentation escalate into his head. He feels a wave of dizziness that has nothing to do with the motion of the ocean. The Colonel sips and sets his drink down on a small metal filigree table next to his chair. He coughs slightly as he chokes down his libation. After dabbing at his

Colonel,"Certainly there is something in what you say regarding containment. Because of the immense implications of this find, the utmost discretion is required to handle it's – disclosure to the larger world. But, what makes you think the longstanding institutions of your city incapable of managing this admittedly somewhat untidy affair?"

Brick,"The Navy, university, police, the D.A., the newspapers, like you said; Mankind has experienced an explosion. In technology, in communication, in travel. It's becoming harder to keep secrets in a world becoming smaller and smaller. I'm on your side. Just trying to provide some extra insurance so that a coherent and not too detailed narrative can be submitted to assuage the public that everything is under control."

He lifts his glass in salute and takes another swallow. The bubbles make a clattering noise in his head as they dissolve on his tongue and a slight mist coalesces before his eyes.

Colonel,"There is enough in your recommendation and your personal character – and in this I concur with our byzantine behemoth, which is intriguing in it's seemingly inexhaustible invention - that I will take a few minutes to seriously consider your proposal."

Brick takes a deep breathe and replies,"So, safe passage for my client and myself and some sort of down payment on my."

The Colonel seems to attempt a small smile in reply.

Brick squirms a bit in his chair at this at this, but the motion brings Pines into the edge of his vision and an idea strikes him,"I suppose your daughter is no security risk as she says she's never allowed ashore."

The Colonel gives a small snort of dismissal,"The girl is spoiled, exacting, smart and manipulative." He leans in slightly, one corner of his mouth pinched in what could be a smirk,"Did she plead to be rescued from the clutches of the 'mad scientist'?

Brick keeps his eyes on the Colonel, but turns his head slightly and notices Pine's nostrils quivering with repressed emotion.

Brick,"She sounds positively mutinous. She must have some redeeming feature for you to keep such a potentially volatile liability around. It must be the paternal instinct in you."

The Colonel's face droops and a crease of annoyance joins other furrows made of time's protracted passage,"If I seem sinister as a father, Mr. Brick, it is because any man who indulges in parenthood at my age deserves all he gets."

Brick risks a glance at Pines who seems to have become even more agitated. Brick shrugs casually,"It's no skin off my nose. I've got enough to deal with in my life without having to complicate it with someone's scheming siren."

Pines lurches into view, stiff-legged and stops between the conversant pair. Leaning slightly forward from the waist, he drags one hand from his jacket pocket; it is tightly gripping a .45 automatic pistol. The other long-nailed hand convulses at his side as he intones in a low growl, strangled by white-hot anger,"Tell him to lay off about Baby. I'll fog him if he don't and no ancient power can stop me."

Brick smiles with amusement and gratification,"You're in the real wild west, now son. Let's not concern ourselves with this pulp rag desperado."

"Now, Louis, you should attach so much importance to these things...." For the first time, the old man seems discomfited and his bony shoulders work apprehensively underneath his gown.

"Then make him lay off. I've listened to all the crap from him I'm going to take." The spindly figure sways, his eyes burn with a yellow malevolence and Brick could swear his beard stubble thickens.

The Colonel flaps a mollifying hand at the resentful factotum,"Now, now, Louis." He settles back a little wearily into his chair,"Louis actually doesn't like to carry guns, I make him. Otherwise his natural proclivities are just as effective, but a little too... idiosyncratic."

Brick, "He seems quite animated on the subject of your daughter."

Colonel,"She is not without a certain allure, which young Louis here finds amenable. I, as her guardian tend to have a more dispassionate view. You may judge which is the more reliable."

He motions to pines to attend him,"Now, if you will excuse me, I shall take a little time to consider your proposal. Should we come to a mutual understanding, when might you be able to deliver the item?"

Brick,"I can't get the piece until daylight."

The Colonel purses his lips, then replies,"That is acceptable. And arrange for it to be brought here." Then he adds quickly,"What I have in mind is that it would be best for all concerned if we did not lose sight of each other until our business has been transacted. Until, later, then."

A crew member comes stumbling through the sand and foliage, doffs his sweaty cap and stands waiting for orders.

"Please escort Mr. Brick to his cabin," the Colonel rasps and then begins to cough in earnest. He clutches his handkerchief over his mouth and nose and waves at Pines and thumps the hand rest on his wheelchair. The sailor bows and replaces his cap on his head and adds in a servile tone,"This way, sir."

The squat sailor leads him up the port side of the ship. Along the way, Brick makes note of the lifeboat access on that side. He casts he gaze aft and he can see that they are out in open waters, past the Golden Gate. The coppery construct is becoming shrouded in mist, a titanic harp among the clouds, it's anti-collision lights casting pink halos. The Point Bonita lighthouse sweeps a spotty stream through the encroaching fog.

As he goes to close the hatch behind him, Pines suddenly appears, bows with a certain insolent mockery and gestures for Brick to hold the door,"Wouldn't want to have a man overboard."

Pines enters, then gestures for Brick to cast his glance at his bunk. He complies. As Brick crosses to his berth he finds a freshly pressed suit laid out for him on the mattress.

Brick picks up the suit with one hand and samples the material with the other,"Nice," he moves his hand to the lining and checks the label,"Cuba, nice. And my size."

Pines,"So, when does the boss tell the chef to serve the main course?"

Brick looks up at Pines as he crosses to a mirror mounted on the bulkhead and holds the suit up in front of himself for inspection,"Can't get hold of it til dawn."

Pines frowns, then shrugs. He turns and exits the cabin. He opens the hatch to reveal Darya in the act of knocking. He gives a snide smile and continues to hold the handle as she steps into the cabin. He slides out and closes the hatch behind hm without further comment. Brick sees her in the mirror, but does not immediately turn to address her,"You were the one who clocked me from behind so Terranova could slip out." He can see her eyes flicker in the reflection as he turns to face her.

"I had to stall for time. I did not know just how much you were willing to overlook about your encounter with Senor Terranova in your pursuit of the bat. I'm sorry, I had to play along, don't you see?"

"And the phone call to get us out of the office before the fat man's messenger could reach us."

Her eyes drop to the deck and she nods as she moves slowly forward to him. "yes, I was desperate to keep it from getting to you before – before

I could explain." She is in front of him now, looking directly up into his eyes. Hers are dark and liquescent with entreaty,"I only resorted to such drastic things, because I didn't want you to get really hurt or – or...." Her open mouth trembles and she looks away.

"Or end up like Walt, since that seems to have been the actual motive. We're you calling on behalf of the Colonel, since it seems to have been Pines who did the job on Fat's muscle."

She grabs his arms,"Oh, no, Lloyd. Please, believe this, if nothing else: I have nothing to do with these, these monsters!"

"So, they're the monsters", Brick drawls in mock astonishment."It seems to me, that practically everyone in this screwball case is some kind of chimera."

Darya,"No Lloyd, I'd never work that on you. Please don't hurt me. If you'll help me, I'll just go away...."

Brick,"That's not something that's in my power to accomplish right now and even if I did, there's too many loose ends that could come back and haunt me." He looks at her with red eyes and a mouth twisted in anguish. He grabs her and bends her back," Let's just make it this; I shouldn't because all of me wants to – wants to say to hell with the consequences and take it on the lam, just the two of us." The cords in his neck throb in time with the vein in his temple.

Brick,"It's easy enough to be nuts about you. But, then most everyone seem to be unable to help themselves in your presence, but I won't follow in Walter's or anyone elses footsteps to the gallows." He holds her at arms length,"Have you had a chance to use it on the Colonel?" He releases her.

A small crease appears between her eyes as she asks in a small voice,"So, that's it? I'm on my own?"

"I won't play the sap for you or anyone else" Brick,"I'll make the best deal I can to get us both out of here intact, but if you have nothing to contribute at least don't gum it up."

He chucks her under the chin and assumes a devil-may-care grin,"I'd miss you if they chop off that pretty little head of yours, or stake your heart or what ever it is they do with whatever you are."

For the first time, she responds as if truly hurt; her eyes well up and her lips tremble as she blinks back tears. In spite of himself, Brick finds himself both exasperated and shamed, his color rises again as he grasps her hard by the shoulders and in a strained tone he hisses,"If what I've said before isn't enough, then let's just make it this: When your partner's killed you have to do something about it. Personal feelings aside, we're in a dangerous racket and it's bad business to let killers get away, bad for every detective everywhere. Almost as dangerous as clients who keep their real agenda to themselves."

Darya,"What will you do?" Her eyes have a wild tinge, she asks breathlessly,"Something wild and unpredictable?" She doesn't seem to register the tightness of his grip. She stares, fixedly into his eyes, her face a barren mask.

Brick,"Maybe."

They hold each others gaze in a panting daze. She raises her arms to embrace his. This makes his cognizant of the force he is using and his grip relaxes, but does not relinquish it's hold. Slowly, she extricates herself from his arms while holding their mutual gaze. Then, wordlessly she crosses to the hatch and opens it.

He watches her go, his pulse slowing, his breath easing. At the threshold, she pauses and offers,"Be careful, Lloyd. After all you seen, you think the worse that can happen to you is death?"

Brick,"Live and let live, but we may be talking about people going from just being a meal ticket to a meal, and that's where I definitely get off. See you at the captain's table."

She takes her leave slowly, their gaze still locked on one another. Once the hatch closes behind her. Brick stares for a few moments, then retreats to his bunk to roll another coffin nail.

Brick is staring at the cabin porthole. Through a haze of cigarette smoke he discerns a figure move past outside. After a few moments, it returns from the opposite direction. It is wearing a fedora and trench coat. It passes by again: it seems to be pacing.

Brick sits up in his bunk and swings his legs so that his feet hit the floor. He experiences some slight vertigo and rubs his hands over his face several time. As he rises, the cabin seems to increase in it's rocking motion. He sits abruptly again, grips his head in his hands as images and sounds come rushing through his mind: "Ancient power, ancient power…" repeats over and over, Pine's voice increasing and diminishing in volume like an erratic pulse as the Colonel laughs manically while images of him unwrapping his head, swathed like a mummy flicker by in a jagged rush.

As he attempts to rise again, the floor turns to quicksand, with each rolling of the ship, he sinks deeper and deeper. He claws ineffectually at the grit finding it is littered with cigarette butts. He looks up to see a familiar trench coat sleeve with a hand extended towards him. Brick struggles to the bulkhead, trying to crawl-swim his way. The two hands strain to reach each other, the distance expanding and contracting with the careening of the ship. The hands grasp at each other, fingers fumbling in desperation. Then, his partner's hand abruptly withdraws leaving Brick clutching a sliver of wood between thumb and forefinger. The stick as a strike anywhere tip on it.

Brick sits up abruptly in his bunk. Breathing heavily, he slowly takes in his surroundings and rubs his eyes with the heels of his hands. He slowly moves to a sitting position at the edge of the bunk, takes a few moments to consider the evaporating shreds of images from his dream. Then, he takes a few deep breaths, stares for a few moments at the suit he had draped over the chair earlier, then rises and crosses towards it.

Brick is shooting his cuffs and adjusting his tie when there is a brief rap of knuckles on the hatch and Pines dicks his head into the cabin,"Let's go, gumshoe. Time to get served."

9

Every Crackpot

Once inside the dome, Pines leads Brick to the dining area, then promptly disappears, leaving Brick to take in the mise-en-scene: The Colonel is seated at the head of the table, the only discernible change is that his aba is now a pale, eggshell tone. His daughter sits at his right hand, her gaze directed downward to her plate. She is dressed in a pale blue halter-top dress with a ruched bodice to ostensibly accommodate the heat. The effect made her already alabaster skin seem almost translucent. There were four other seats, but they were empty as Man Fat and Terranova huddled together at the other end of the expansive table which could easily support a dozen more guests.

The humongous denizen of Chinatown was decked out in his usual fez, but his monumental frame is now encased in a pale green seersucker suit and Testoni Moro shoes. His stout companion is tugging at his Van Heusen comfort collar shirt. He is draped in a light gray seersucker suit with wide lapels that only serve to accentuate his conical contours. Brick quickly scans the scene to find Darya also removed from the table, but hovering near her own little grove of potted palms nearby.

She is arrayed in a dark blue sarong with a fuchsia flower pattern which gathers around her neck leaving her shoulders bare. Her lustrous hair falls in a single dark wave gathered over her left ear with a small barrette ornamented with small gardenias. She looks quite apropos among the tropical plants. Brick loosens his own collar and walks towards her. On the way he makes note of the chafing dishes, wine carafes, silver ware, candelabras both on the table and on stands arranged around the dining area.

From out of the engulfing foliage, Pines now appears as head waiter/ butler in white tie and tails. Brick's face contorts with amusement – the slinky goon looked about as dashing in formal dress as Buddy Ebsen.

Turning to the elaborately set table, Brick notices that there is no place setting for the Colonel. The Colonel notices that he notices,"You will excuse me, I dined earlier. My condition requires a specialized diet." His daughter's head drops lower and her shoulders hunch slightly, Brick observes.

"But, please," the aged explorer gestures expansively,"I would be remiss if I did not exhibit a proper regard for my position as host, dine first. Business can wait." And with that he claps his hands and indicates the chair closest to him for - "Miss Markov". Darya hesitates only a moment, then moves to the proffered seat. Brick steps in and holds the chaise for her as he speaks into her ear, sotto voce,"Let's hope it's not a last supper."

"Gentlemen," and the Colonel indicates to Man Fat and Terranova to take the remaining seats at the sides of the table. This implicitly leaves the one chair at the end opposite the Colonel open. The Colonel gestures appropriately and Brick slowly steps around and seats himself in it.

Pines moves to the chafing dishes set behind Darya and Terranova and begins to serve up what turns out to be an elegant seven course meal. As the meal progresses, Brick takes more and more notice of the behavior of the participants: he watches as the Colonel's daughter picks listlessly at each dish before her. Man Fat, on the other hand savors each mouthful while Terranova takes no more than a bite or two of each thing set before him, then drums his fingers impatiently on the tabletop. Darya, eats daintily, leaving only the smallest portions of the major dishes.

After the palate cleansing sorbet and a few minutes of watching the floor candelabra sway too and fro with the gentle swell that rocks the ship Brick raises a glass in salute to the Colonel,"Veuve Clicquot champagne, Dresden china – glad to see something from there will survive. Is this Tiffany silver? I'm not sure I recognize the pattern." He holds up a soup spoon to the light for closer inspection.

The Colonel seems to preen a little in his response,"Sterling, and the pattern is known as 'Persian'."

Brick,"I'm curious, since it would seem you take pains to have the best of everything about you, why you would be interested in coveting an item that seems to have been an abject failure at it's intended purpose – as fantastical as the story is."

The deep-set eyes of the Colonel flicker with something more than annoyance, but he covers quickly,"I'm sure your city's resident expert," he nods towards Man Fat,"has explained to you the seemingly singular nature of this artifact. My whole career has been one of exploration and discovery. This would be the crown jewel of my life's pursuit."

"Of course. Your interest is purely academic. Others seek it for their own material ends," Brick also nods to his fellow diners. "It's just that – with all of the unique experiences of the past few days, imagine my chagrin if I were to actually give someone a key to human extinction."

The Colonel seems about to respond, when Man Fat sets his drink down a little more forcefully than he intends as he interrupts,"Gentlemen, we are not here to debate ancient beliefs, but to contract business. Once the Colonel has authenticated the artifact, it will be the pieces de resistance of his monumental collection, which will tour the globe to great acclaim and undoubtedly, profit."

He settles back and adds in more congenial tone,"Speaking of which, the Colonel has iterated your offer, well sir, as to that -"

Brick,"Oh, there is an addendum – a fall guy."

A befuddled silence ensues as the other guests look from one to another. Finally, Terranova mutters flatly," A fall guy…."

"Don't you see? The criminal justice system has to have a victim – a suspect they can stick for those murders and the assault, even. The newspapers have already started to flog city hall about the recent shootings. The wheels of justice are turning, gentlemen. They need lubrication."

Man Fat,"Indeed, and there is certainly something in what you say regarding containment." He casts a glance at the Colonel who simply stares straight ahead with a scowl.

Brick casually brushes at his lapel,"I'm doing a public service, but there's no reason to consider it strictly a favor."

Terranova shrugs and nods,"If you are good at something, never do it for free."

Colonel,"From what we've seen and heard of you, I think we can leave the handling of the police to you, all right." His face remains a glowering mask of distemper.

"Monahan's public persona is at stake, I need to give city hall such a neat little package, that they'll take the nag without a glance at his choppers."

Man Fat looks to the Colonel, who looks away. The behemoth shrugs and lifts his glass and inspects it as he relates,"Our intelligence kept close tabs on the young sailor and notified us of his contact with the professor which was a more fortuitous happenstance than one could ask for as it gave us the perfect opening to acquire the precious object without having to directly involve the Navy of the United States. Our attempt to obtain the prize from across the bay was successful, but somewhere in the transportation to my safekeeping, it disappeared." He swirls his glass lightly and takes a swallow.

"And it's assumed that my late partner had something to do with it."

Man Fat, "He was in charge of security for the evening."

"And being mistaken for me, he was assumed to be a breach in security."

"Perhaps," Man Fat acquiesces with a small gesture,"Something like that was bound to happen under the circumstances what with the night, fog, and the two of you being about the same size. ..."

Brick mutters to himself,"Too slick for his own good...."

The Colonel cocks a hand to an ear and leans forward,"Pardon?"

Brick gives a small shake of his head,"Nothing. Then a couple of days later it shows up on my doorstep courtesy of your Japanese bodyguard, turned into Swiss cheese. An inside job, it would seem, but why would he bring it to me and who tried to stop him?"

Man Fat,"I assure you I have gone through the organization and have no reason to believe the conspiracy was more than the parties already indicated."

"So, you figure I was part of this "conspiracy".

Terranova,"It only makes sense that one would try to get it without paying," he shrugs.

Colonel,"If we were to entertain this antic idea of yours, whom would you suggest we sacrifice?"

"Easy,"Brick responds with a smirk. He jerks a thumb at Pines,"Those numerous bullet holes would fit laughing boy's profile just swell. I mean, he must've shot at least one of the two."

The Colonel scratches absently at his throat,"I've ordered Louis to be more discreet. But, considering his natural proclivities, it seems overkill is to be expected no matter the method."

Brick,"I'll take that as an admission of culpability. Shouldn't be hard to persuade the D.A. to keep it simple on your say so."

Pines' eyes bulge and his face pales with surprise, then darkens with anger as he glares at his employer.

"And ass long as at least one of his weapons matches ballistics, the D.A.'s office should have enough -" Brick continues until -

Colonel,"But, my dear fellow, if I even thought for a moment of agreeing to what you propose, what would keep Louis from telling anyone who'll listen to him all about us and the -"

"Who is going to believe a story like this one, even leaving out the more problematic notions of the supernatural? And, considering the pull the two of you have," he nods to man Fat and the Colonel,"I'm sure you've had experience keeping uncomfortable questions from being asked before."

Pines glowers at the Colonel and shaking with anger he growls,"Are you really gonna let this flatfoot-"

Brick,"There's still enough of the Sidney Town mentality here that someone as brazen as I can get away with sowing reasonable doubt in people's minds to the point of mania."

The Colonel waves his feeble looking extremities in a placating fashion,"Now, now, Louis. You shouldn't let yourself attach so much importance to these things. We are hearing Mr. Brick's proposal merely out of common politeness -"

Brick leans over the table,"After they get a load of his kisser, they'll get a conviction standing on their heads. And as for motivation, well a what's another couple of notches on the belt of the Triad?"

"You bastard, get up and shoot it out. I've taken all the riding from you I'm going to take!"

Pines has pulled a .45 automatic pistol from his tail coat and holds it aloft with one hand. The other hand flexes in frustration by his side. Brick notes the extreme hairiness of his hands seem to have increased and the nails have darkened and thickened into points.

Brick,"Is this the first scam you've tried to pull? What am I dealing with here, amateurs? This is the real world. Not ancient Egypt, not the middle of the Pacific Ocean, this is my town and I have no intention of folding up my tent, willingly or otherwise."

Man Fat rises from his seat and approaches the Colonel. He leans down with a cupped hand and whispers slowly into the antediluvian ears. The Colonel stares hard, his brow contracted with resentment.

Brick smirks,"Six, two and even, they're selling you out, fido."

In a voice hoarse with emotion, the hireling cries out,"All right! You asked for it!"

He starts towards Brick, his gun hand rising, but the Colonel reaches out reflexively and grasps his other arm with a strength that surprises the gathering,"Louis, don't!"

Both ladies start in alarm and Pines gapes back at his employer which causes the old man to let go with an abashed expression on his face. Once released the gun man then turns his attention back to Brick and stalks forward, stiff-legged, his gun hand again moving into a firing position when the Colonel calls out again, this time in a low, warning tone,"Louis…."

But, this has given time for Man Fat to have maneuvered around behind and now Pines is grappled from behind. They struggle at first, then the mammoth Tong chieftain lifts the squirming, gangling figure off of his feet. With a bone-crushing bear-hug which elicits a howling of pain from the pinioned hood and the gun drops from his benumbed grasp.

This only causes Pines to struggle more frantically and in the process a cracking, grinding, sound like a cooked fowl being disjointed by eager hands is heard. Before everyone's gaze a transformation takes place: a Bulldog jut extends Pine's lower jaw, fierce canines extend to crease his upper lip, hair sprouts like a time-lapse film of a fecund alfalfa field across his features. He reaches up with his now extended claws and swipes at his tormenter and knocks Man Fat's fez off. Blood trickles as the large man laughs with then challenge.

But, that is enough for Terranova to join the fray. The thick-set figure trundles forward and launches himself at Pine's knees and the three combatants go down in a heap. Darya moves cautiously and reaches down and picks up the fallen weapon. Everyone else stands stock still in stupefaction as the writhing mass seems to wind down in it's contortions. Pines' flailing gradually ceases as he loses consciousness. The extremity of his features also regresses, leaving him pale and shivering, but recognizable.

The Colonel's daughter stands, riveted with her hand over her mouth. Man Fat and his ally slowly peel themselves away from the now unconscious figure and slowly stand and brush out their disheveled outfits. The Colonel glowers sadly at the prone figure and says softly,"You can have him."

His daughter keeps her hand over her mouth, but turns her head and looks wildly at her father. Then she drops her hand to reveal a mouth down-turned in disgust as she glares balefully at the scene, then turns and runs away into the foliage, her eyes brimming with tears.

"Senor Terranova, please be so kind as to inform the chef to wait to serve the dessert as Mr. Brick has an important phone call to make. And send a crew member to escort him to the bridge", the Colonel mutters as he sinks back into his chair.

Man Fat frowns at the downed minion,"Isn't it a little dangerous from someone in his 'condition' to fall into the hands of men who might want to find out if -"

Brick steps in and raises his voice to an authoritative level,"The D.A. can have him sedated for the kangaroo court trial and he need never be seen again. Maybe they'll cut a deal with the Agency and have him vivisected. Either way, he's history."

Except for the roll of the swell, no one moves or makes a sound. Brick glances about at his fellow diners: Terranova looks disgruntled and looks to Man fat who in turn turns to the Colonel who will not meet his gaze. Darya looks on, her mouth a grim line of determination, but her brow is creased with apprehension.

"No one in authority wants to admit that there are beings like them out there." He gestures to Pines and Terranova as he moves towards his client."Same rationale as Foo fighters. Or, blame it on the nuclear age. Or Nazi or Kempeitai experimentation."

He stops in front of Darya and reaches for the pistol that she dangles, seemingly unconsciously at her side. She looks up at him, startled as he takes the pistol from her. He turns back to the company just in time to see Man Fat replace the fez on his head with one hand and simultaneously produce, seemingly out of thin air, a small, black pistol in the other,"I'm afraid I must insist...."

Brick marvels that his cumbrous finger can fit in the trigger guard, but it does. He smiles at Man Fat and tosses the pistol into the pot of a small palm and raises his hands, all benign good nature. Man Fat's focus stays on Brick as he addresses his stocky partner,"Senor Terranova, if you would be so kind as to escort Mr. Brick to the bridge."

When they reach the bridge, Terranova raps on the hatch, then swings it open and gestures for Brick to enter which he does. Once inside Brick notices the Captain is on the bridge, leaning on elbow at a console. His chaperone gesture to a phone near the radio console. Brick crosses over and picks it up. The Radio man nods OK, points to Brick, removes his headset and then himself to other side of the deck.

Brick lifts the handset and speaks into it,"Operator....? Get me Prospect five, five five two seven."

Brick pulls away the handset away from his ear to alleviate the pop and hiss of the phone connections, his attention drawn to the shop's Captain who now seems to be gently snoring. The phone is picked up after the thirteenth ring,"Hello?"

Brick,"Hello, angel sorry it's late...."

Lorna's voice is thinned by distance and static,"I wasn't quite asleep...."

Brick,"Everything go OK with Maclane and company?"

Lorna,"I told them what you told me to tell them and nothing more. It was easy for them to believe the phone call had something to do with it and that you were chasing down a lead."

Brick,"Good. Now, here's the play, partner," he leans more intimately into the handset and lowers his volume,"In our Holland Post Office Box there's an envelope with my scrawl on it. Inside is a ticket to the Pickwick Stage parcel room. You'll need to get Tom to help you bring it out."

Lorna,"Tom? Does that mean that you've -"

Brick,"It means you two are the only ones I can trust right now." Even through the static and distance he can hear her sigh,"I hope you're not being too slick for your own good. All right, see you soon."

Brick,"Tell him Tom I hope to have a nice package for him, too. Hell, bring Maclane if he wants. I'll hand you over now so you can get the directions. We seem to be anchored well inside the three mile limit." He passes the handset back to the radio-man and stalks to the hatch. He takes one critical glance back at the Captain. He smells gin. "Never trust a gin drinker", he muses as he exits.

As Brick closes the hatch to the pilot house, he turns to see – Darya. Wrapped in a dark woolen coat with a fir-trimmed collar, her hair mantled in a blood-red scarf that whips frantically in the dark ocean's night breeze. They stare silently for a moment, then Darya nods her head. He turns to follow her gesture to see Terranova hovering close behind. He smirks and steps towards her as she asks, "Still open to the highest bidder? What makes you any different from -"

Brick steps into her and takes her by the upper arms,"Don't be surprised if I'm not as mercenary as I seem. It can do wonders for keeping the enemy off balance. Now, both of us sitting under the gallows. I've no reason to believe that anyone will make it out of here alive, if either the fat man or the mummy gets their mitts on the goods, but I've got to buy time and maybe a little luck to see that we don't end up walking the plank."

Brick's turns his gaze to the open water, his mouth is pinched and turned down at the corners and there is pain in the shadows that surround his eyes. He grasps her arms harder,"You came to us because you knew Walt was involved with the bat. I won't bother asking how, and when you heard Walt had been killed you figured you'd need further protection, so you came back to me."

She looks up at him and grasps his arms in return, her eyes liquid and pleading,"Yes, but, it wasn't only that. I would have come back to you sooner or later. You're one of those rare men who -"

Brick,"Don't bother bringing up my character or your feelings, it's poor salesmanship. I'm not sure why the Colonel has kept you around, unless he's as unsure as I am of you and your -"

Just then, the Colonel's daughter approaches. They both turn their heads and pull slightly back from each other. The young lady just stands, pale and shivering, watching them both in a leather topcoat, her own head bare, her flaxen locks damp, but the stiff breeze still manages to carelessly stir the tendrils around her face. She crosses to the two of them and slips her arm into Brick's. She frowns and jerks her head dismissively, indicating Terranova should scram.

The gnome glares dubiously, but shuffles slowly away, casting a glance backwards as he retreats. Then Miss Casper also takes Darya by the arm,"Come with me. Both of you," she says somewhat thickly. Brick and his client share a glance. Brick shrugs, then gestures for his client to follow as the daughter leads them aft.

When they reach the boat deck, the Colonel's daughter takes them up the steps past the lifeboats. She comes to a stop in front of the exhaust vent closest to mid-ships, bends over and laces her calf-skin gloved fingers together and looks at them expectantly,"Come on," she nods at Brick."Give us a hand," she then addresses to Darya. Brick looks at his client and shrugs, then steps into the proffered boost up as Darya reaches up to help steady him.

With small grunt, Brick hoists himself into the cowling of the funnel and as he perches himself he begins to discern voices drifting hollowly up from below,"What the -" Miss Casper forestalls his query with an abrupt shushing gesture and points emphatically to the interior of the vent. Then she leans heavily against the towering object. Brick frowns, but as he shifts himself a little further into the bell-like opening, he can just make out the intonation of the Colossus of Chinatown -

Man Fat,"He's a man in search of a hidden truth."

The Colonel's voice rattles like loose gravel in the metal chute,"I don't know that the larger world is ready for the truth. He'll might be able to settle for redemption, if he were to get out of this alive."

Man Fat,"Miss Markov has proven to be more reliant than expected."

Colonel,"More of a hindrance, than a help, but still...."

Man Fat,"Yes, it would be most helpful to know her true alliance...."

Colonel,"She is a supernumerary with seemingly limited resources, whoever has engaged her, I think our own triad with City Hall will inure us to any immediate repercussions."

There is a slight pause, then:

"Eventually this artifact will change everything we know about life and death," Something like a sigh seems to escape him,"We live in an era where age-old beliefs such as gods and demons are denigrated as delusions being held by the simple-minded, tsk, tsk."

"Hm. Well, certainly who could ever have envisioned that a remote atoll in the middle of the Pacific ocean would one day be smashed to atoms," Man Fat responds in an assuaging tone. "Well, sir, here's to a fair bargain and my we both profit greatly from our endeavor." There seems to be a clink of glasses and maybe even a dry growl from the Colonel,"In any case, the bat will soon be here and the others will at last be a minor annoyance."

Brick decides he's heard enough and signals to the ladies that he is coming down. He hops down between them and brushes off his hands and coat. He takes both of them by the arm and conveys them back towards the greenhouse,"We'd better get back before your father releases some flying monkey to fetch us."

Just before they re-enter the giant terrarium, Brick brings the trio to a halt. He spies Terranova standing sullenly nearby, hands deep in pockets, shuffling his feet impatiently. Turning to the ladies, he rests a hand on each of their shoulders and says softly,"Don't be surprised at what you may see and hear in there. It's my intention that the only deserts served tonight are just ones." The ladies look to each other, then Darya turns back to Brick and nods. Miss Casper swallows and sways slightly becoming even paler than before. Brick frowns and shakes her shoulder. With a sharp intake of breath, she looks up and smiles weakly. Then she squares her slim shoulders and opens the door to usher them back into the hothouse.

Rounding the foliage into the dining area, the tableau before them presents them of an image not inconsistent with the Spanish Inquisition: in one chair, slightly removed from the table, Pines lolls, head down, bound to the back of the chair. From this attitude it is impossible to discern his state of consciousness. Man Fat sits in another chair, his head now swathed in a makeshift tea towel bandage. Terranova makes his way to his side. The Colonel still exhibits a sullen mien, dabbing at his mouth with a handkerchief again as he gestures for everyone to be seated.

Man Fat nudges Terranova in the direction of Miss Casper. The young lady stands by her chair, weaving slightly. Terranova is nudged again, looks askance at his employer, but slowly rises and makes his way, grumbling to himself, to help her be seated. He takes her arm as she sinks unsteadily into the chair. Then she takes a big breath, tosses her head and nods at the gnome in gesture of acknowledgment and dismissal.

As Brick takes helps to seat Darya, he remarks,"I see my addendum has been agreed to," and nods, indicating Pines. "Now, what about a little earnest of my share of the future profits?" he asks as he crosses to his own chair.

"Well, sir, as to that…." the Colonel produces a white business size envelope and feebly flips it onto the table. Terranova eyes it covetously, but after a moment, slides it on down the table within Brick's reach. Brick takes deliberately takes his time picking it up and opening it. When he extracts the contents, he fans them out evenly on the table top: crisp, new, one thousand dollar bills. Ten of them. He looks up and says mildly,"We were talking about a lot more money than this."

"Yes, we were," the old man agrees. "But, this is genuine coin of the realm. With this we should be able to purchase a small grace period to insure we are free from any legal entanglements while we complete our process."

Brick's upper lip twitches sourly,"I ought to have more than this."

Man Fat starts to explain,"Of course, sir, you understand this is simply the first payment. Later on there will be -"

"I know, I know,"Brick chuckles, interrupting his host. "Later there'll be millions. Sure, you can't sweeten the pot, say fifteen grand?"

The Colonel folds his hands together and smiles amiably over them at Brick,"I tell you frankly and candidly and on my word of honor that ten thousand is as much cash as I could access at this late hour."

"But, you didn't say positively."

The Colonel's smile broadens ever so slightly,"Positively."

Brick pouts and shakes his head sadly,"That's hardly equitable, but if that's the best you can do…."

He sullenly sweeps the bills off of the table back into the envelope and tucks them away in his suit pocket.

"I would be remiss if I hadn't asked you, Mr. Brick, but did you happen to notice any hieroglyphics on the receptacle?" The Colonel's hands start to slowly twist over one another.

Brick nods,"Sure. I didn't have the time to inspect them very closely, but I do recall seeing some figures etched around the top. Why? Is there some significance to -"

"Oh, no. Nothing, nothing," the Colonel demurs as the tempo of his hand wringing begins to quicken."Only I would know the secret of their translation in any case."

Brick,"Maybe we shouldn't open it," offers casually with a shrug. All eyes turn to him, except for Pines.

Brick,"It might actually lose value. There's definitely something inside, but maybe like Schrodinger's cat it may be best left to conjecture."

"Ha!", Man Fat barks. "Very amusing, sir, but let us stay within the realm of -"

"Man, himself has unearthed this divine instrument meant to align us with the gods!" the Colonel glares at Brick with the menacing gaze of a raptor.

"There are more things in heaven and earth than are dreamt of in your etc, etc," the fat man waves his hands dismissively. "Be that as it may, when can we expect delivery?" Man Fat leans on the table, casting an anxious glare at the Colonel.

Brick's gaze rests on the Colonel, but he replies to the sometime Asian,"Can't get it until dawn or a little after."

The large gentleman also keeps his eye on the colonel, but leans back in his chair,"That shall be satisfactory; we don't have to be out of each others sight." He turns to Terranova,"Miss Casper? I believe your father could use your calming company." Brick notices Pines lifting his head slightly as if scenting the air.

The Colonel, however, pays no notice. His palsied movements have taken on a careless languor. His eyes seem to have enlarged and his head waves about slightly like a child's balloon as it tilts back and he gestures to the night sky, momentarily held at abeyance by the lights arranged for the evening's repast,"Man has split the invisible, unleashing forces he can barely control or understand. The world has been witness to man igniting the very atmosphere, bringing down black rain like stinking pitch. Heaving promontories and Poseidon's realm into the air in a matter of seconds and yet these archaic bits of folklore have no place in your scientific world." He glances briefly about, acknowledging the extraordinary individuals present as prime examples of his assertion.

Man Fat,"It's obvious that tonight has been a great strain on the Colonel's health, perhaps we should all retire until-" he begins to rise from his seat at the table.

"I've been shadow-boxing with reality since this caper began, but I understand the motivations of these three," Brick gestures to the other dinner guests."But, you Colonel, actually believe in the ability of this device." Brick absently scratches his head for a good Clarence Darrow-like casual gesture of equivocation,"A majority of the civilized human race managed to keep itself from blowing up twice in the last thirty years, but maybe the clock is ticking, I don't know. I'm just not sure I want to be responsible for speeding it up any."

Man Fat,"It seems our private detective feels he has a public obligation; what the Japanese call 'giri'. Don't tell me a man in your profession can actually afford a conscience? Especially one so easily influenced by the rantings of an old man -"

The Colonel shakes his head with distaste, seemingly oblivious to the turmoil of the others,"A man always with an ear to the wall, an eye to the keyhole, always on the outside looking in. How can he be expected to comprehend the big picture?"

Man Fat moves to the wheelchair as if he would propel his now seemingly ludicrous business partner out of earshot,"It seems the Colonel has over extended himself -"

Grumbling, the Colonel pushes himself forward in the chair, dismissing Man Fat's attempts to placate or mollify the now agitated host,"In case mankind finally does itself in, a strain of it may be preserved! For better, for worse. For posterity. And who's to say it might not even be an improvement," a dry cackle rattles in his throat. "An unnatural selection abetted by man himself", the Colonel nods in appreciation of his own assessment."Almost as if he unconsciously wished another chance to continue in spite of his seeming desire for total self-annihilation as you, yourself asserted."

Mr. Brick, it becomes unfortunately clearer that any knowledge of this evenings affairs must never leave the confines of this ship."

"What about our deal?"

Man Fat,"It was your idea to feed the system someone to assuage the masses, to consecrate their illusion of safety and justice."

Terranova,"Why *shouldn't* we leave you holding the bag? I'm sure the police would happily toss in the chum once you've hit the drink."

"Do the math, Mr. Brick: a war hero in peace time with a head wound and write if off as shell shock. It actually makes for a rather sympathetic angle for the press. Just another unavoidable consequence of the horrors of war."

The giant moves to Pines and snatches a knife from the table,"You may have the opportunity to indulge your unique predilections, yet. In or out?" The gangling brute glares at the entire ensemble with unalloyed malice, but when his gaze comes to rest on the daughter he frowns and drops his head. After a moment he nods assent. Man Fat reaches down and with one mighty stroke, severs the cords that bind Pines to the chair. The big man drops the knife carelessly and moves away as Pines rubs his arms in an effort to stimulate circulation.

Pain is creeping like tendrils up his spine to his head. Brick inhales deeply and leans back in his chair. He looks idly at the fork in his hand as he plays with it and says, carelessly,"You know, it's often through the keyhole that the most important clues to secrets are gathered."

The Colonel's daughter gives a small gasping cry and faints, her head dropping with alarming alacrity to the table. Brick moves quickly to her side and taking her shoulders, leans her back in the chair. Doing so gives Brick a powerful whiff of acrid fumes arising from her now open mouth.

"Laudanum," he mutters as he peels back her eyelids and checks her dilated pupils. Dark spots gleam sickly on the front of her dress. Brick opens it to find – white flesh criss-crossed with thin red lines and dots where she scraped and punctured her torso in order to stay wake. A fork falls from her now nerveless hand. He looks closer at the arm and discovers, something else: a subcutaneous bulge that runs along the inside of her forearm: a fistula.

"Don't! Can't let.... not.... father....", she gasps as she twists in her chair in frustration then subsides again.

The pain in his head now is plaintive. A very ugly thought suddenly coheres in Brick's mind. He looks incredulously at the dinner's host,"I'm going play a hunch that your desire for this transformational trinket is quite personal. No wonder everyone says you came back a changed man, Im Ho Tep. To you it may represent a kind of Fountain of Youth. Looks like you're tapped out here."

Everyone at the table freezes. Mouth's agape, Man Fat, Terranova and Darya stare in wordless awe at each other. Pines' snorts and his lips slowly peel back to divulge a trap-like set of teeth which part slightly as his tongue snakes out and tickles an elongated eye-tooth. He moves towards the head of the table.

As Brick tries to make the young lady as comfortable as he can in the chair, Pines nudges him out of the way with a growl and drapes his own coat over her. Then he gives his client a piercing glance as he resumes his seat. She catches his gaze and lowers her head, her eyes sliding amongst the other characters with studied intent.

"But – but, what you are proposing is preposterous. It's a lunatic as – as…." the Colonel's enormous partner sputters, but the seemingly implacable host merely stares straight ahead, his eyes wavering slightly with reminiscence and opium," This vessel has obviously become decrepit, the bat device may obviate need," he nods at his daughter."Don't forget, I was considered the first physician. In my time we acquired much knowledge that has since been lost to time and man's carelessness. And just the past few years, the almost exponential explosion of scientific knowledge has only added to my remarkable store."

Brick,"I don't know about anyone else, but I could use a drink", he and Pines exchange surly glares, then Brick moves to the well stocked trolley. "Anyone else?" he queries as he arrives and starts to pour. He looks up, "You never know, it may amount to a last request. He is greeted with a strained silence."Well, hell…."he takes the bottle, pours two fingers into a tumbler and drinks.

"Sealed in by high priests of the royal necropolis. Entombed alive for the sacrilege of attempting to steal what should have been rightfully mine as would befit my status as Chancellor, second in line to the King." The desiccated figure leans forward, hands gripping the armrests, it's eyes on a past only it can see, "Inscriptions of the sacred spells to protect the soul on it's trip to the underworld were chiseled off of my sarcophagus. They thought it an ironic touch that I should be condemned to death in both worlds by a coffin of my own making. But, the fools were so anxious to carry out their insidious crime, that they failed to notice the secret compartment I had designed for my eventual revival into this world", he gives a small snort of derision. "After such treatment and betrayal, how could I ever 'rest in peace'?"

Brick has poured himself another drink and now raises the glass in salute," Well, best of luck to your venture, gentlemen, but I must insist on your honoring deal to the extent of -"

Man Fat,"That is hardly logical or equitable, sir. No, No, I do not think we can do business along those lines. He looks a little sadly at his host/partner,"I'm afraid, this little twist in the story makes it imperative that none of this reaches the ears of others, whether there is any validity to what we've heard tonight or -"

"Fools!" howls the ancient entity,"Inside that compartment was a document as powerful as the bat: the scroll of Toth. Yes, the same invocation Isis used to raise Osiris from the dead!" He thumps the armrest on the wheelchair for emphasis."Ten years trapped in that tomb! Left for dead by plunderers tipped off from our own camp! Only one of the party left alive. Barely. What else could Colonel do, but read the portion of the scroll of Toth incomplete as it was, damaged by the tomb raiders?"

Terranova looks anxiously at his kingpin who jerks his head in a gesture suggesting a tactical retreat. Brick catches this and sidles his way back towards the table as the explorer continues unabated by the discomfort of his guests, "It allowed us to survive by 'merging' our identities. The strain has made this vessel frail. The only thing that has kept us alive was the last of the Casper family blood line." He heads lolls a little sadly towards the collapsed figure of the daughter, hunched in the chair.

Brick moves next to his client and says sotto voce out of the side of his mouth,"The only deal making here tonight is with death."

A muffled 'thud' sounds from aft and the whole ship shudders. Everyone freezes. There is a deep rumble in the below decks like a querulous digestive shift. The greenhouse guests look anxiously about and at each other. There follows a distant, agonized moan of stressed metal and then the structure is suddenly raked with beams of light. The inhabitants shield their eyes and squint into the glare. A

Brick ducks low and scrambles towards Darya. Once he reaches her he grabs her by the elbow and yells to her over the now blaring klaxon alarm,"We should get to the lifeboats!" They look around to see: Im HoTep remains seated, implacable, hands folded across his chest, eyes closed murmuring ancient charms and spells, the space that held the prominent mass of Man Fat has become considerably vacant. Brick snorts with derision and amusement as he sakes his head,"Swell lot o' thieves."

Brick grabs Darya's hand and they start for the entrance, when she tugs him back,"What about her?" She nods towards the still inert form of the daughter. Pines is hovering over her, but it seems that the current situation has only brought out the worst in him as he struggles with another transformation before their very eyes. Terranova suddenly appears before them, pistol in hand,"Not so fast, I intend to get my hands on that treasure, even if it means -"

Suddenly, Darya interposes herself between Brick and Terranova. The blunt figure snarls at her,"Your tricks don't work on me."

Darya,"What makes you think I'm trying?"

She reaches down and plucks Brick's untouched drink from the table and back-hand tosses it into the gnome's face. He sputters and gasps, rubbing his eyes. Brick grabs at one of the candelabras and thrusts it at the distressed dwarf, flames erupt and cast a small blue aurora around the flailing figure. The pistol flies from his grip and clatters out of sight. Brick grabs his client's hand and they make a break for it.

Pines has lifted the slim blonde into his arms, but has now fully transformed. He stands, slavering over her as she blearily wakes and with a gasp discerns her predicament. He seems to regard her with a mixture of desire and agonized concern. She starts to squirm in is arms and presses against his chest with her hands as she weakly cries out.

Darya jerks Brick to a halt almost before they get started. She pulls him to face her,"We can't just leave her." He looks from her, back to the fairy tale couple; beauty and the beast. He sighs, nods to his client and hustles back towards the table.

The slim blonde is fading in her struggle to free herself from the hirsute arms of the hoodlum, but more importantly, they have made no progress towards an exit. As Brick approaches, Pines looks up at him and snarls. Brick reaches into his jacket pocket and clutches – the fork he found in the girl's grasp. Pines does not change his hold on the girl, but thrusts his head and snaps at Brick who tumbles forward and stabs Pines in the ankle with the silver cutlery.

Pines' head snaps back towards the heavens and he emits a tormented howl. The girl drops from his convulsing arms and lands on Brick. He scrambles up from underneath her and starts to drag her to her feet. Pines rolls on the deck, holding his ankle and yelping in pain. The silver has caused a violent reaction with his blood and a smoking, bubbling black ooze exudes from between his clenched fingers.

As Brick finally gets the semi-conscious girl to her feet, they both turn to see Pines as he begins to weaken and revert to his more socially acceptable form. The girl practically swoons in Brick's arms, so he hoists her up as best he can on his hip and they turn towards the exit.

They only get a few staggering steps before a smoldering apparition appears before them: Terranova. He has shaken off the effects of the flames, and stands confronting Brick, blocking his egress once again. His clothes smoking, his singed features twisted, his mouth contorted with anger and pain, he stalks towards Brick, confident that the detective will not abandon his charge. Brick lowers his shoulder and anticipates the impact as the miniature, pyramid-shaped goblin lurches at them, which sends the three tumbling backward.

Brick scrambles back up. The girl is now lying unconscious, a battered doll, splayed on the deck several feet away. As he clutches at his aching shoulder, the looming hulk of Terranova rises in front of him, once again. The gnome seems bound and determined to make sure they all go down with the ship.

Suddenly, Darya springs up from behind the portly imp and drags at his coat collar until the burnt and rent material impinges his shoulders and arms. He bellows and twists about, flinging her off of him and into one of the potted palms. As he continues to thrash about, rending his garments further Brick moves to Darya's side. She raises shakily up as he reaches her. By now Terranova has stripped off the binding apparel and closes in on them with deadly intent.

Darya grasps Brick's arm in alarm, then suddenly shifts her gaze and tugs at his arm,"Lloyd!" He follows her wide-eyed stare and discerns the dull gleam of a pistol handle poking out of the scattered soil from the plant's container – the one he had stashed away earlier. He leaps and snatches the weapon out of the soil just in time to level it at Terranova who halts his advance.

Another explosion, this time much closer and louder. The ship shudders as dark, acrid smoke begins to roil into the greenhouse. More wracking groans from the superstructure as the ship begins to list slightly to port. Terranova smiles at Brick and lifts a potted palm by it's trunk with one hand and looks about to hurl it at Brick, when Brick smiles in return and aims the pistol up towards the glass ceiling. Terranova's smile vanishes and his face crumples into bewilderment.

Brick pulls the trigger in rapid fire action – glass explodes far over the gnome's head and the air is a plummeting torrent of gleaming glass. One shot shears the chain holding a transom, which flips down and collides with the panes below sending a cascade of lethal shards towards the prone figure of their unwilling hostess. Brick and Darya gape in distress at the sight of the helpless and heedless lass beyond their ability to reach before -

In a flash a scraggy figure leaps into the space and drapes itself over the insensate blonde as the crackling shower slams into the deck waves almost drowning out the agonizing screams of the squat Spaniard. Both Brick and Darya stare with dread at the sight, debris filtering and twinkling through the air in the slashing beams of light. Something shifts fitfully under the glittering veil on the deck. Brick aims his gun at the swaying form that rises from the debris – Pines, and in his arms the still unconscious girl. The ragged character sways forward towards Brick, pierced by at least half a dozen large shards of greenish glass, that wink in the light in contrast to the red-black blood that oozes sickly over his shaking form.

He and Brick collide and he drops to his knees after leaving the girl in the detective's arms. Breathing heavily he looks up at Brick and his mouth twists into a sneering smile. Then his eyes roll back in his head and he pitches face forward into the deck. Brick looks down, his mouth a grim, taut line as he mutters, "Good boy."

Beyond their field of vision in the debris and smoke, Im Ho Tep, finally stops his arcane utterances, unfolds his arms and glares about him at the chaos and destruction. Then, he leans forwards, arms bent at the elbows, spindly hands firmly gripping the chair's arms, shuddering. The chair rocks back and forth unevenly, then: the wheelchair splinters under his grip as he rises. He thrusts the remains of the chair in his hands to the deck and stalks briskly and determinedly forward.

"Let's get the hell off this Flying Dutchman," Brick pronounces as he grabs his client by the arm and peers ahead to find the path of least resistance out of the enclosure. As they turn to go, a hysterical crewman goes wailing past them. Just as he rounds a small palm he is clocked in the head by a Jungle Carbine. As they watch him drop in his tracks, Brick raises his pistol, then they both freeze in astonishment as a petite blonde all in black steps out of the foliage.

Brick gapes at his associated but addresses his client, "Tell me you're seeing this."

"Women Accepted for Volunteer Emergency Service. Guess the powers that be considered World War Two to be an emergency so; covert Navy intel in Hawaii," Lorna explains as she uses the back of her hand to push back a stray lock of hair out of her eyes.

Even in the distraction of the chaos Brick manages to be staggered by the totality of what he does not know. "Special forces?", he infers.

"Absolutely. Lose lips sink ships, right? You'd be unpleasantly surprised at the amount of classified gum-flapping a G.I. on shore leave in a Waikiki bar will gladly declare if he thinks a girl is khaki wacky."

Brick, "And here I was all concerned about dragging mother's lamb through the gutter."

Two G.I.'s crash through the palms and trot up to Lorna. Brick squints through the drifting smoke and recognizes the square-jawed profile of her cousin. The young blonde sailor salutes Brick with a smile, the other square shouldered fellow turns to his cousin, "We've got a small problem, one lifeboat is away already."

"Any forty on the 'Rara Avis', Captain?"

"No joy." comes the response. He looks at Brick, "Get the ladies to lifeboat. The 'naked warriors' can mop up here." He turns to Lorna's cousin, "And get someone to the bridge to eighty-six that damned horn."

Brick looks quizzically at the glistening figures hustling away through the shadows and strafing glare of the chaotic scene and it occurs to him that the men appear more like swaddled amphibians in their baggy green suits than warriors.

Brick, "'Rara Avis'?" He turns to his partner.

"The code name for the device," Lorna shrugs,"You know how the military loves their code names."

Brick,"But, I thought that the one -"

Lorna shakes her head,"That was a decoy. It seems that the Colonel had acquired the actual device from Walt before it could get to Man Fat. The Navy thinks he wanted all the players here in one spot to eliminate the competition in one fell swoop. You were in the fat man's shop. He had replicas of the jar made. Maybe he meant to hide it there in plain view, or use it to throw others off the scent, or make tchotchkes for the Embarcadero."

"And the Navy thinks it made it's way here", Brick sums up. "Speaking of which, how long has the Navy been behind this whole SNAFU anyway?"

"That's a very cynical question from a fellow service member," she pouts.

"I could get even further and suggest that the on board fireworks are a result of the underwater demolition team being careless with matches, but let's save that for our exit line."

"Really, Lloyd. Who else would you suggest to deal with this?" She shrugs her shoulders. "The Russians?" She shakes her head, "Nazis, Japs, hell even the Chinese but, this…. who could ever have expected this?" Lorna waves disconcertingly at the prostrate forms of Terranova and Pines under the debris. "Follow me." She nods towards the exit. Brick and Darya hold up the girl as best they can between them and Lorna leads the way through the now maze-like minefield of debris.

As they emerge from the double doors of the foyer of the atrium, the alarm ceases. Brick and Darya wheel the young girl over to the ship's gunwal as Lorna covers them. Now that the klaxon has stopped there seems to be almost a vacuum of sound, then the shuddering of the sinking vessel reasserts itself. Lorna looks about, then gestures with her weapon,"Can you launch the craft yourself?"

Brick straightens up and bushes his hands together,"Carry on smartly. The Navy expects every man to do his duty."

Lorna shakes her head,"See you on shore, partner." And with a rueful smile, she turns and trots away into the night. "Stay here", Brick admonishes Darya and she nods in compliance. Brick trots to the stairs and clambers up to the boat deck where he releases the arm and swings the lifeboat out over the side into position.

Darya clambers into the craft as Brick ascends the stairs two at a time. Then she holds out her arms to receive the crumpled figure of Miss Casper as Brick lifts her into the boat. Brick moves to the pulleys to start the descent as Darya secures the girl. She looks back up at him as the boat descends unevenly with much jolting of the craft and calls out to him,"What about you?"

"I'll be right behind you!", he bellows over the cacophony. He continues to lower the boat into water, hand over hand with the rope when a strong arm wraps itself around his neck and right shoulder. He Snaps his left elbow back to catch his assailant in the ribs, but the attacker's strength is formidable and he can only struggle to the point where he can see Im Ho Tep's malevolent face perched over his left shoulder. The ancient North African's strength is prodigious. He lifts Brick off of his feet and just as the detective feels himself being hoisted over the railing another explosion shatters the bulkhead behind them and hurls them high into the night air and then crashing into the chill Pacific Ocean.

The cold seizes Brick immediately, causing his chest to contract and his whole body starts to shiver violently. He scrambles towards the surface when something catches his eye -

The burning flames of the sinking ship sift through the dark waters, the ambient light catching a glittering 'T' of gold tumbling deeper into the frigid depths. He twists in the water, reversing his ascent, but like a dagger of the mind it leads him further down, just out of reach. The shining object keeps falling away into the murk, the cold and lack of oxygen almost obliterating his senses and impinging his movement when – he is suddenly grabbed from behind, by the shoulder. He is yanked around to face – Im Ho Tep, his mouth a snarl of effort and enmity.

"Not again!" Brick thinks as the all too familiar attenuated fingers wrap around his throat. He grasps the narrow wrists and presses with his knees against the sunken chest of his uncanny adversary, but he feels the cold leeching into his limbs and his mind and eyesight are starting to dim. His breath spurts out of his mouth and nose in clots of frantic bubbles. His hands can no longer hold a grip and like his consciousness, begin to drift away from his body, when – his right hand flails and slaps against something hard, cold and sharp. His hand seizes the object reflexively and Brick starts from his swoon.

He starts to bring his hand around, when he feels his adversary jerk away from him as if snagged by an enormous force. The dimness of the deep water only allows the back-lit impression of two forms struggling with their hands at each others throats: one, the skeletal figure of Im Ho Tep entangled with the bear-shaped bulk of Man Fat. Brick feels the cold seep in again as the adrenaline of the struggle wears off and his body shivers violently and his vision darkens from the edges. The fez of the large not-Chinaman sails past his face and he feels himself starting to float upwards and that somehow a little shut-eye right now would be just the thing.

10

The Egyptian's Hand

Swooshing and swirling, burbling echoes buffet his ears. He feels his head twisting around in a cold, churning current. He feels a grinding sensation in his chest and his breath comes in short, sharp stabs. The sounds in his ears become more distinct; voices echoing in and out of range:

Iva,"Sometimes I think I know what you're going to say and other times...."

"Other times?" he hears his own voice reverberate.

"Other times you're just a stinker."

And the voices swirl away in a clamoring, slurring jangle of a holiday tune, until:

Lorna,"Tarnish is not necessarily fatal."

"It is little enough to be allowed the grace of redemption", Darya enjoins. Their voices quaver with distortion, but the words are perfectly discernible. However, in what may be a response to their assertions, there seems only to be a loud grinding sound, like boulders murmuring together, then -

The remote sound of footsteps echo become louder, closer until they shuffle to a stop. The snap of a lighted match and the flutter and crackle of flames silhouette a rugged masculine profile under a snap-brimmed hat. A large exhale of smoke follows, and another drag on the cigarette, the crinkle of the burning paper increasing the eerie gleam on the visage as the eyes slide towards Brick," Kudos, kid. You've made the big time. Always knew you had it in you. Hell needs to be fed and that can happen by making it here on earth. After all, if you can't trust your partner, who can you trust?"

The face of his late partner turns to him. His pallor is decidedly green. He tips his hat and shuffles away. He passes a lone streetlamp, it's globe hanging pendulous, wreathed in fog. The figure seems to be humming as it eventually is swallowed by the darkness. Are those tattered wrappings trailing behind this apparition?

Brick starts to follow the familiar figure, but his legs seem mired in ooze and with each step he seems to sink deeper into the pitch. He tries to call out, but the sound seems to dissipate as soon as breath reaches his lips. He stops moving forward and his descent seems to slow. He reaches out his arms trying to find purchase or assistance, when -

Darya's face appears over his right shoulder. He can suddenly feel her weight on his back, her legs wrapped around his torso. She raises her right hand and his eyes follow. The object in her hand glimmers with gold and a barbed sharpness in the dimness. She looks at him,"Gee Lloyd, if you're that afraid of dying..."

And she brings her raised hand down, hard into his chest.

Brick wakes with a gasp. In his mind, his attempts to concentrate are like gears slipping. Thoughts careening into each other like bumper cars and recoiling beyond his ken.

His breathing feels labored, but not constricted. He slowly opens his eyes, but the glare of light overhead causes him to grimace and turn his head away. He swallows hard and risks opening his eyes again. Windows swim into focus as he squints into the violet light of dusk. Condensation on the window smears the glare of the anti-collision lights of the Golden Gate bridge. He is still seeing it from the west, but why from Land's End? His gaze sharpens and he focuses on the colonnades that frame the view and recalls the bas relief figures of the Art Deco ziggurat of the San Francisco VA Hospital.

Brick tugs at the neck of his hospital gown. He's sweating. An ultimate 'episode'? He swallows hard and his throat clicks with arid tension. Two, squat, familiar figures also coalesce into view: the District Attorney and the Chief of Police. Brick almost bolts upright not only in surprise, but in some primal instinct of ablution, before his injuries and own contrary nature bring him up short, wincing. It is only then that he registers the disconcerted expressions and constantly flickering of anxious eyes of his illustrious visitors. His glance follows theirs as he hears heels clicking across linoleum tiles.

Darya in a black wool two piece knit dress, with a narrow leather belt and rib-pleated skirt slinks across the room. Her long dark tresses, with bangs now covering her forehead like a sable fringe, sway as she crosses the room and hovers next to his bedside.

He stares at her, trying to retrieve his last memory of her, but his thoughts careen about like untethered cargo in the hold of a tempest tossed ship.

Lorna's voice drifts into his right ear,"Im Ho Tep's vessel is at the bottom of the ocean. Best left there." She steps into his field of vision. She is dressed in high-waisted, pleated, olive green pants, cinched with a narrow leather belt and a yellow, yoked blouse with a gold Federation of Women's Clubs pin over her left breast. She crosses her arms as she settles behind and looms over the shoulders of the two male authority figures, who seem to squirm slightly and clear their throats.

Darya,"These two esteemed community leaders are here to not only offer you their best wishes in your recovery, but to assure you that the Colonel's insidious plans have been effectively thwarted by the exemplary and joint efforts of both San Francisco City Hall and the United States Navy." She sits provocatively in the chair next to the bed and crosses her shapely, dark-stockinged legs. The eyes of the two males again dart about as they attempt to not take the bait of her allure.

"And, it's their job to see that the public is reassured that their city will spare no resource to see that their citizens are convinced that all levels of their government is responsive to their needs. Thank you again, gentlemen for your co-operation and concern." And with that Lorna leans forward and gives each man a small, squeeze on their respective shoulders. Both act with fitful alacrity, and rise. The Chief fumbles his gold-braided cap on and almost salutes. Then both men hurriedly shuffle out of the room, sputtering best wishes and apologetic assurances of further compliance and contact as Darya holds the door open for their hasty retreat.

She leans on the frame of the open doorway and continues to watch the pair as they scuttle away down the hall. Brick can hear their muttering and the squeaking of their Florscheim's fade into the distance. Then he calls out to Darya,"Is their craven exit do to your supernatural charm?" He is shocked that his voice comes out a cracked, dry rasp. Darya turns to him and with a brow puckered with concern, she holds an index finger up to her piquant lips and urges him to hush.

But it is Lorna who speaks next as she maneuvers her way around closer to his bed,"Men are more susceptible, but she has learned how to finesse women, too. Over time."

Darya leans with one hand on the door frame,"Because of my power over men, other females become jealous, so I often have to try the aggrieved sisterhood angle. But, sometimes mere sisterhood isn't enough. Sex can be thicker than blood, for instance." Her eyebrows lift as if in amusement, but her mouth remains serene in it's luster. "One reason it was felt that you were worth sustaining was because of Lorna. Originally you were considered as expendable as your partner, but plans changed after you showed some backbone to my influence."

Brick turns his head and gapes at his partner. She merely ducks her head and tucks her chin into her chest and a blush settles over her freckles and her dimples appear.

Darya," You got me to spill while I was on the job. Very unusual, almost unprecedented in, well – a very, very long time. It was proof of your adherence to justice – a last test. Lorna always told us you'd come through. She always believed in you."

"Us?" Brick squawks again. His throat pains him and he settles back into the bed as Darya nods to Lorna to exchange places with her. As she speaks, she starts towards the bed as Lorna slowly backs away.

Darya,"Osiris is not sure that the time has come in spite of humanity's penchant for escalating ways to send themselves to his realm. And it is his will that he controls the device that he himself consigned. Osiris wanted to be able to create as well as destroy and he felt that Im Ho Tep would not hesitate to use it, before it was 'perfected'. It was taken away from Memphis to be further from Im Ho Tep's grasp, eventually the item's whereabouts was lost for many years after an aborted robbery attempt after it left the continent."

Lorna,"U.S. intelligence wanted it, but needed to obscure the trail. What looks SNAFU was has actually given them the cover they need."

Darya,"In any case they could now legally claim it as salvage U.S. water or no."

Brick closes his eyes as if in pain and sinks further back into the bedding,"So, after all my efforts at justice, I end up owing the capo di tutt'i capi of the underworld."

"Not exactly," Lorna says as she takes up station in the doorway and peers out. Into the hallway.

Brick opens his eyes in bewilderment.

Darya,"They can only claim it if they find it. And they are not the only ones still looking."

Brick turns his head towards her,"You mean he's -"

"Hades needs to be fed and man has been making hell on earth in an accelerated fashion lately, so he should be preoccupied for some time." Darya leans casually on the head board and inspects her fastidiously polished and manicured fingernails,"The reason you are still here is because Lorna told me of your intriguing plan. After far too much time watching what havoc patriarchy has had on the history, there may now be a chance to help correct that mistake."

"Oh, good," Lorna calls out to someone in the hall."Come on in. He's finally awake."

Darya steps aside slightly to clear Brick's line of sight to the door,"But, since it's still a man's world, all agreed that you would not only be a more than suitable figurehead, but someone of your character is essential in seeing our little experiment in restoring balance to the scales of justice."

Just as she finishes Lorna steps back inside from the door frame and smiles as Iva and the Colonel's daughter enter the room. His partner's widow is turned out suitably in a black, long sheath of a dress, the long sleeves pushed up to the elbows, a wide leather belt cinched at the waist, the hem just below the knee. Her hair in a black turban with a glittering mauve jewel set in the middle. She sports large silver bracelets and hoop earrings. The young lady is decked out in a two piece, brown checkered skirt and jacket ensemble, with a black turtle neck sweater and black beret out from under which her icy blonde mane flows.

They all stand in the room, four sets of vivid eyes bore into him. He feels a small panic well up inside as their stare seems to cause the very room to reverberate with fervid tension.

Brick gasps,"What is all this?"

"This?", Darya responds. She leans down and coos in his ear, her breath an ambrosia of promise, "The, uh, stuff that dreams are made of."

The others smile at him. Their sharp, protracted incisors wink in the western twilight's last gleaming cast through the sweating windows.

About the Author

A longtime writer of plays, screenplays, and poetry, he finally decided to start a novel, but during the research phase, he discovered many other possible story lines that seemed too intriguing to ignore. He has worked in the entertainment industry for decades as an actor, director, and writer, and although always stimulated by the collaborative process, he finds the relatively solitary pursuit of writing to be the most challenging.

Printed in the United States
By Bookmasters